The Fortune Cake

Hope Dahle Jordan

A sudden change in plans, a broken window, a rock painted with a hideous face and a threatening message . . . Jenny's summer changes from a dream to a nightmare.

Jenny discovers a painted rock under a window in the dining room. Its vicious message, addressed to her father, a juvenile court judge, terrifies her. The fear of this man who seeks revenge on her father, the loneliness at Loud Lake, the growing affection for her retarded cousin and the pangs of first love, are poignantly captured in this story by an author who has won high praise for her taut style, timely themes and superb mastery of suspense.

Talk About the Tarchers

"Beth Tarcher's mother, who had never finished high school, had decided to go back and complete her education and become a teacher . . . The story has a mild love affair, a good balance of home and school interests, and a sturdy mother-daughter relationship . . ." *Bulletin of the Center for Children's Books*

The
Fortune
Cake

The Fortune Cake

Hope Dahle Jordan

Lothrop, Lee & Shepard Co., New York

Also by Hope Dahle Jordan
Supermarket Sleuth
Talk About the Tarchers
Haunted Summer
Take Me to My Friend

This book is for one young girl,
PAULA ANN JORDAN . . .
and for two young boys,
JIM and ANDY KELLMAN
who swam with me at Horseshoe Park.

chapter one

Finally—the morning we'd been waiting for!

I'd come downstairs to an early breakfast with my parents. For months we'd been anticipating this day, and I'd been looking forward to two whole weeks of being on my own!

"It's hard to believe you two will be having lunch tomorrow in London," I told them.

My mother's eyes drifted over me. She has dark, glowing eyes and chestnut hair, with gold in it, which she wears long and coiled on top of her head. "Wisconsin doesn't seem snug from the world the way it did when I was young."

I was surprised by the uneasiness in her voice. Only now did I notice that she was clutching the handle of the electric percolator with such rigidity that her knuckles had whitened. Was she still afraid of flying, despite what she said?

I glanced from her to my father.

He is County Judge Harold Jonsson of the children's court. A tall, erect man with iron-gray hair, he's my idea of a really fine person.

But now when I actually looked at him across the table I noticed that the smile around his eyes was absent. I had the feeling I wasn't going to appreciate his next words.

I didn't! "We've changed our minds about your staying alone in this house while we're gone," he said in his official voice.

"But you *promised.*" I dropped my toast onto my plate. "If I'm grown-up enough to go off to a big university next month I surely can be trusted—"

"We trust *you,* Jenny," my mother said, slowly spreading lingonberry jam on her bread. "We don't trust the world around you."

Now what? I slumped in my chair. "There isn't a safer place than Rockwood."

My father emphasized, "As it *used* to be—even five years ago."

I retreated into a line of reasoning which, because it irritates him, I usually try to avoid. "You hear an ugly case in children's court, and you're extra strict at home with me."

In the uneasy hush I could hear a *ping* in the kitchen

8

as water dripped into the sink. My mother put her hands to her forehead. "Now I wish we'd insisted that you come with us."

"No, no." I was so upset that I was utterly frank. "I don't want to poke along to a family reunion."

The Jonssons who had emigrated to America and the branch of the family that had settled in Australia were getting together in Stockholm, Sweden, this month to celebrate the ninetieth birthday of Grandfather Jonsson. To top this, my father had been invited to present a legal paper at an assembly in London. This was quite an honor, and everything happened to dovetail beautifully. The London conference was scheduled for just five days before the big party. There'd been weeks of anticipation, heightened by letters from Sweden. Everything was set for this morning . . . *and now this!*

Did their last-minute decision have anything to do with me and Dan Mengers? All along that had seemed to be an unexpressed stumbling block. None of us had come right out with it, but ever since they'd started planning their trip there'd been a subtle change in their attitude towards me and Dan, and our closeness. They'd even hinted that I not have him alone in the house while they were away. To help my mother's peace of mind, I'd gone along with the idea, although this was practically Dan's second home.

I didn't want to take the glow from my parents' trip. But neither did I feel I should knuckle under to last-minute jitters, which would spoil my few remaining days with Dan before we had to part for our separate colleges—mine in nearby Madison, Dan's in Massachusetts.

"You'll only be gone two weeks," I reminded them. "And with Aunt Hertha right across the street ... *well!*"

Generally, I'm inclined to avoid my mother's widowed sister. Living so near us with her two daughters, my aunt has managed to keep an unwelcome eye on me all the time. Openly and often, she had chided my mother for allowing me too much freedom.

I winked at my mother. "*Maybe* I'll meekly do as Aunt Hertha says. Maybe *not*—if she tries to go to Loud Lake before Labor Day weekend."

My father sighed audibly. "You may think you've had too much of the lake already this summer—"

"I do, I do." During all of June and July I'd been bitter about what I felt was unnecessary separation from Dan during our last summer before college. Weekends, when Dan came to the lake, weren't enough. Yet I'd tried to keep busy. I'd practiced shorthand and typing, and I'd begun sewing clothes for a fall wardrobe.

Such a waste of good time!

Ever since I can remember, there's been Dan. He's the boy in the next block down Sawyer Street who used to pelt me with snowballs, but got mad if anyone else did. We've strung along together for years.

My father leaned forward. "You know, I've told your

aunt that our cottage is completely hers while we're gone."

"But she said we'd go there just a couple of days the last weekend." I was ready to explode. All summer I'd been counting on these two final weeks in Rockwood. "She *can't* change her mind now."

Sighing, my mother pushed back her chair and started to pick up her breakfast dishes. "Hertha's allowed to change her mind. *She* needs a vacation too."

This was too much. In my dismay my eyes were misty as I glanced from one parent to the other.

My mother turned towards the kitchen.

"I'm sorry, Jenny Lou, but you'll have to do what she says." It's serious when she adds the *Lou.*

Suddenly my father glanced at his watch. "Gretchen, do you know what time it is? Jim'll be along any minute to drive us to O'Hare."

"I know."

They hurried upstairs, but I didn't move.

11

chapter two

As I slumped down again on a dining-room chair, I couldn't remember when I'd ever felt so frustrated. Overhead, the squeaks in the ceiling of our old house told me how rapidly my parents were moving about in their bedroom. They probably were locking their suitcases now, and soon they would be gone.

But it no longer made any difference. Now I'd just be under Aunt Hertha's control instead of my parents'— and she was a lot stricter.

At that moment a whistle drew me to the double door which leads to our side yard.

"Good morning, Dawn," I called to the girl who was dragging a red wagon loaded with dolls and bunnies, all bedded down in a system that only my small cousin understands.

Dawn is the younger of Aunt Hertha's two daughters. Around her neck she wears a ten-cent-store whistle on a heavy corded chain. Strangers guess her to be about eight, but she is really twelve. She is retarded. My mother told me that during Dawn's birth her brain was probably cut off from oxygen—just long enough to be damaged. The doctor had to work fifteen minutes to make her breathe.

She is a lovable, gentle child with a heart-shaped face framed by thick dark hair. It takes a while to realize how totally expressionless that pretty face is. Her eyes, large and gray, are shadowed by long lashes. She raises and lowers them with no awareness of how she snags at my emotions.

She and I are good friends. Two years ago I made up my mind I'd teach her to read and write. Rockwood schools couldn't give her the special attention she needed, and Aunt Hertha had scoured the state for help, with no luck. I set up a pattern: a certain date, hour, and place. You have to be definite with Dawn. She can't cope with the unusual. I learned to repeat, repeat, repeat . . . but once my young cousin has memorized anything she doesn't forget.

There are times when I get terribly discouraged by her slowness. But working with Dawn has made me decide that I want to teach retarded children after college.

Dawn is always formal. Now she said, "Good morning, Jennifer." She held up a sheet of lined paper. "I've brung my letter."

Automatically I said, "I've *brought* my letter," as I accepted her weekly report.

Some time ago, realizing she had to have an accomplishment, I'd come up with the scheme of her writing a letter once a week, telling me what she'd been doing. Actually, it's a form letter with one or two comments of her own. I wrote the original; she pretty much copies it.

She treasures the colored stars she earns.

I knew exactly how the letter would begin.

"Dear Cousin, It is a warm day. The wind blows from the south. It is 82 degrees."

Always the weather first, parroted from the television report. Then what she'd eaten at her last meal. The behavior of her doll family, a trip in the car, news about her sister Tracy or her mother.

As I stared at the childish square letters I bit my lip. She had written, "Tomorrow I go to the lake. My sister who is Tracy will go. My mother will go. My cousin Jennifer will go. The man will go. My aunt and my uncle will fly in an airplane."

Tomorrow—oh, no—not tomorrow! And who was "the man?" Could she possibly mean Dan? For an instant a wild hope soared through me that my parents and Aunt Hertha had cooked up some secret, appeasing plan . . . but immediately, sanity returned.

14

I studied the pretty face, but the large gray eyes were contentedly blank. "Dawn, what man?"

Something like distress touched the corners of her mouth. "My letter—won't I get a star?"

I untangled the whistle around her neck. Sometimes I think I've learned as much from tutoring Dawn as she's learned from me. At the top of the list is that I must always put a happy melody into my voice. This best keeps the door open to the girl I'm trying to reach.

"You will get a *gold* star," I told her.

Lifting her pretty face, unnaturally pale in spite of August's blazing suns, Dawn stared at me in such a fixed manner that I realized there was something she knew that she simply hadn't the ability to communicate.

I knelt to her level and she put her face close to mine. Her voice had the soothing quality it has when she's talking to one of her dolls. "You won't be alone when Uncle Harold flies away." Uncle Harold is my father. "Mama will watch you all the time."

"I'll just bet she will," I groaned.

A helpless, baffled feeling came over me. Dawn's innocent letter was loaded with references to Loud Lake. Even *she*'d been in on the change in plans. Why wasn't I consulted? My mother said she trusted *me* but not the rest of the world. Was she classifying Dan as the rest of the world?

15

Suddenly I realized I was still in my pajamas, and if this was going to be a difficult day I'd better dress and face up to it.

I curled my toes in the grass as I watched Dawn drag her wagon across the street. "I won't go with Aunt Hertha," I swore to myself. "I'll figure out something. . . ."

chapter three

As my parents drove away, they didn't give the impression of two people looking forward to a nice vacation. A pang went through me. My mother was wearing a new suit of nubby blue wool. She looked lovely, but she was biting her lip as if she were thinking of dozens of last-minute details.

She waved. I hoped she couldn't see the bleak expression that was probably on my face. Never, never had I expected to feel like this at the sight of them driving away. Noticing that Aunt Hertha, Dawn, and Tracy were waving from their front door, I turned and ran back into the house and up to my bedroom.

A few minutes later, I walked to Northcote's Hardware Store, where Dan had a summer job. I hoped he'd have time for a break. I simply had to consult with him

17

about my exile to Loud Lake. Dan isn't a talkative person, but when he speaks he says something, and what I needed now was advice.

When I came into the store he noticed me right away. We went behind the building where there were gnarled trees and flat rocks.

"Dan, it's crazy! At the last moment my parents have come entirely undone."

"What happened?"

"All of a sudden they're overwhelmed at leaving behind their only child. They're trying to park me full time with Aunt Hertha at the lake."

I guess what I wanted was an outburst of protest from Dan, but he arranged his face into thoughtful lines and ran his hand gently through my hair. "What have you done to scare them?"

"Nothing," I protested. "Really, they never did think it was a good idea to let me stay alone in the house. I just wore them down with my coaxing. You know, they try to treat me like a grown-up, but when it comes right down to it I'm still a little kid to them."

He made a sympathetic sound. "You and Tracy," he said, and the corners of his mouth quirked, "in the same small cottage."

I don't know why, but my cousin, a year younger, and I just don't get along. We've lived across the street from each other all our lives, but we've kept that street between us.

18

"You can see they're desperate. Normally they'd do anything to keep us two separated."

"Well, Tracy's the least of our worries now," Dan said.

I sat up straight. "What do you mean?"

"I think I've got a buyer for my car. We're getting together tonight. I'm leaving so soon, I can't turn down a prospect."

I looked up at him—lean, confident, strong, settled on a rock as comfortably as if it were a sofa—and moaned. "But Dan, if I *have* to go to the lake, how could you come up weekends without your car?" Unhappily I thought of another complication. "And what about the Big Hollow Harvest Festival on Labor Day?" I cried. I always had fun at the Festival. We'd planned on it for weeks.

"I'll arrange something by Labor Day," Dan promised. "Right now, the snag is these two weeks. I'd planned on your being only a block away, but if your aunt—"

"I won't go. I'll think of *something*." I was afraid I was going to cry in sheer frustration. Instead, I jumped to my feet. "Your break must be over," I said. "I've got to go."

chapter four

Not until I was ready for bed, that first night alone in the empty house, did I have a chance to think. I'd kept busy all day since my parents left, and I'd eluded Aunt Hertha's supervision entirely. But now I felt lonely.

I reached for the telephone. Dan answered on the first ring.

"Hi," I said. "Did you sell it?"

"Almost. At least, we're still bargaining," and he told me more than I wanted to know about the snow tires and the faulty distributor. He was almost sure they'd come to terms tomorrow or the next day.

Maybe it was selfish, but I'd been hoping the deal would fall through. All I could think now was that there'd be no more long talks like this. Telephoning

20

between here and Loud Lake would be long distance.

When Dan asked about my schemes for avoiding the departure to the lake I had to admit I hadn't come up with anything. He seemed as disappointed as I was.

After we hung up, I wandered around the house pondering the problem. The morning paper had been lying on the hall table all day. Sometimes reading the news was a good way to put one's troubles into perspective. Picking it up, I smiled, remembering how long it had been since my father had eaten breakfast without his newspaper to hide behind. In their flurry to get things in order he hadn't even missed it.

I carried the newspaper upstairs.

Propping up the pillows in bed, I was startled to see a headline about Eric Schallen—a name I remembered well.

His had been a difficult case. His trial had given my father grave concern.

At sixteen, Eric Schallen had murdered his father. Eric had wanted to use the family car, over which there'd been constant wrangling, and his father wouldn't let him.

He'd stayed home as he was told, but that night when his father was asleep Eric shot him with a rifle.

His older brother helped him bury their parent in the back yard, and he protected Eric by telling the neighbors that their father was in Florida on business. Their mother had died years before. But people became suspicious and called the police, who had found the grave in the back yard.

Eric had been in and out of trouble for most of his life, and all those years under the supervision of juvenile officers hadn't caused him to change. At sixteen, he was a borderline case: it was up to my father to decide whether he was to be tried as an adult or a child. My father sent him to criminal court.

The case had gotten a lot of local publicity.

"Can't you give him another chance?" I had asked my father, after reading about Eric. "He's not much older than I am!"

"Jenny," he'd said in a gentle but unyielding tone, "the court has to protect the rights of the community as well as those of the criminal. This boy has had many chances. A judge can't be sentimental. Eric Schallen could be a bad example for other minors who think they'll get off easy no matter what they do." In the end, Eric had been convicted of first-degree murder, and his brother was sentenced as an accessory to the crime. Both went to prison.

Now I began reading the latest news about him. My father had been right, I saw.

Eric Schallen had escaped. According to the paper, he had complained of a sore throat. During a trip to the infirmary he had eluded his guard, then vanished from prison. His cellmate said he'd often talked about busting out, and making it to Canada.

I stared into the dark corners of my bedroom. Why had I pitted my snap judgment against my father's studied conclusions? Why had I questioned, and possibly hurt him?

Well, it was a satisfaction to know my father wouldn't have to hear the latest about Eric Schallen until after he was apprehended. Almost certainly, that would happen before my parents returned from Europe.

Dropping the newspaper to the floor, I turned out the lamp over my bed.

chapter five

After a restless night, there is nothing as annoying as waking up to a doorbell ringing persistently. I couldn't ignore it. I slipped into my blue robe and ran to the door.

It was Tracy. Believe me, my heart was not brimming with good will as I swung open the door.

My cousin has never been known for her tact. There are times when she seems to take delight in rubbing me the wrong way, and now was one of those times.

"We're going to the lake today. Are you ready?"

I exclaimed bitterly, "Am I going to be allowed to dress? To have breakfast?"

"Don't blame me. It's Mom who insists we leave this morning."

"Why can't she give me decent notice?"

24

"She *tried*. Finally she fell asleep in the chair dialing your number last night." Tracy shrugged. "One of your marathons with Dan, I suppose."

I didn't intend to discuss my conversations with Dan with her. Or anything else, for that matter.

"I'll be ready in a while," I said offhandedly, and ran upstairs without saying good-bye.

I've always heard that when you're in an emotional state you shouldn't drive. I really shouldn't have been at the wheel. But Aunt Hertha detests driving her car and avoids it whenever possible, and Tracy wouldn't be sixteen until her birthday next week.

Dawn and her dolls sat beside me. She was singsonging. The two voices from the back seat were distracting to me, probably because of my annoyance at my aunt. Why couldn't she realize that returning to the same spot where I'd spent the entire summer was too, too much? That I needed time at home to get ready for college?

There were the new dresses I had to finish.

Of course, I could use Mrs. Cobb's sewing machine at the lake, just as I'd been doing these past weeks. That would be a good way to avoid Tracy.

Suddenly I moaned. In the rush of leaving, I'd forgotten the cardboard box containing my material and patterns.

Aunt Hertha poked me. "You're driving too fast."

Yes, I was. "Sorry."

They resumed a private conversation in the back seat,

and in the mirror I could see Tracy's hands flying around as she talked. It came over me that she was probably as unhappy at having me along on her vacation at the lake as I was to be there.

What a prospect!

Now I was glad I'd forgotten my sewing. It would give me a good reason for having to drive right back to Rockwood tomorrow. How galling, though, to think I'd have to ask my aunt to use her car!

The two of them were backseat driving. Aunt Hertha insisted we take the county road, a blacktop which wound past cornfields and Holstein cows and along the main street of every small town. Tracy tossed her waist-length hair in disagreement. She wanted us to go on the expressway to the Shepard's Run exit, even though we'd have to retrace miles to the lake.

I opted for my usual Route 12. They were so busy arguing that they never noticed.

Couldn't they see how they distressed Dawn when they got carried away in a discussion that, to her, was out-and-out fighting?

I glanced at my young cousin. She hums on one note when she's unhappy, and she was doing it now. A wave of protective love surged through me.

I ran my finger through her hair to make her bangs hang evenly. "Look, sweetie." I pointed to a wooded hillside where a farmer's flock was pastured. "Little Bo—?"

26

"Peep."

"Has lost her—?"

"Sheep."

"And we know where to find them, don't we?"

Appeased, she sagged against me. Before I could start another verse, I saw her long lashes flicker down onto her cheeks.

During our days together, perhaps I could help her overcome her distrust of the lake. When it is perfectly calm, she'll touch her toes to it. But waves of any size terrify her. Now that I would be spending all day with her maybe I could coax her into trusting the water. Certainly, I had to find *some* reason to make the next two weeks endurable.

Horseshoe Park on Loud Lake . . . that's where we've lived all the summers of my life. That's why I sail and swim and water-ski as naturally as I breathe.

Loud Lake is not large and it's not a resort. The only public access is in the tiny village of Loud, where there's a post office, a grocery store with a gas pump in front, and a tavern.

We residents ignore Loud except when we hike along the lakefront to pick up the morning newspaper.

But Horseshoe Park is something special.

There are eleven cottages on the Horseshoe and permanent homes at each end, directly on the lake. We're like one big family. People don't rent out their places, even if they can't be there themselves. Sometimes they lend their cottage, as my father does to Aunt Hertha for a week or two every summer. For most of us it's within easy commuting distance for weekends. On Sundays our long, T-shaped pier at the foot of the bluff is crowded. You can feel all alone on the Horseshoe during the week.

"It sure is hot," I heard my aunt complain.

I pushed my sunglasses up higher on my nose. I'd driven Route 12 so many times that the car seemed to follow its own nose.

Because there's no road in front of the *U* of cottages I guided the car onto the back lawn as close to the screen door as possible.

Dawn stirred.

"We're here, sweetie."

She looked at me blankly. "I'm going to hit him," she said, with sober intensity. "I'll bite him."

I stared at her. How unlike Dawn! Was she having a nightmare? "Who are you going to bite?"

"The man."

After a moment of thought, I touched her chin. "Dawn, do you know about dreams?"

She shook her head.

"They're pictures you see when you sleep. When we have our class together we'll talk about them."

Scooping her dolls into the hollow of one arm, I searched my purse with the other hand for the key to the back door.

28

"*Why, it's open.*" Aunt Hertha, impatient with my fumbling, had leaned against the door and it had opened easily. Surprised, she banged it shut to test it, then bumped it open again. "The lock is set, but it's loose. It'll fall off one of these days."

I tried to conceal my twinge of consternation. Surely my mother and I had locked up last weekend when we'd left the lake? "There's never been a robbery on Horseshoe Park," I murmured weakly.

My aunt, always expecting the worst, asked, "What are we going to do at night?"

"We can latch the screen."

While they made themselves at home upstairs, I took my suitcase into the downstairs bedroom, which my parents always use, behind the kitchen. Slumping onto the double bed, I glanced about the room. The windows were high. My chin would just about touch the lower ledge. Nobody could see in, even though the room was on ground level.

On impulse, I kicked off my shoes and walked over to give the latch another inspection. I fiddled with the door, trying not to make any noise that might arouse my aunt's curiosity. I surveyed the hook. The screen itself was getting rusty.

Quite out of the blue, a wave of genuine uneasiness flooded through me. I shook myself.

I'd better put away the food before I unpacked my

29

suitcase, I decided. Turning towards the kitchen shelves, I stumbled over my portable typewriter.

Impulsively I kicked it.

Two weeks . . . they stretched forever.

Our cottage stands the farthest from the lake of any of the buildings on the Horseshoe. From our wide screened porch at the center rear of the Common we have a view of the oak-shaded lawn, which dips into a hollow before rising to the bluff over the shoreline which, itself, is not visible. Just the roofs of the boathouses can be seen.

All of us are summer residents except Mrs. Cobb, the widow whose year-around home is right on the lake, catercorner to the Horseshoe. Mrs. Cobb is the tearoom hostess at The Clearing, where city women come to shop for antiques and eat chicken salad. Each summer she hires boys to care for the lawns and the Common.

Through the years we've learned each other's habits. Now when I saw her come from behind her hedge and adjust the traveling water sprinkler on the Common, I knew she must be ready to leave for dinner at The Clearing. Holding open our screen door, I called, "Surprise—I'm back! May I use your sewing machine again? I'm still working on my college wardrobe."

She waved a "yes." She protects her throat. It's delicate, she says.

As I came inside, I heard Tracy say, "I don't know why one girl has to have all the luck!"

"Ssssh."

They'd heard the screen door slam and thought I'd gone outside.

"You mustn't talk about her while we're here, Tracy. It isn't nice."

"I'm *nice?*"

I wasn't trying to eavesdrop. Somehow you never imagine anybody talking about you behind your back, and as for Tracy, she's so outspoken I thought she'd say whatever she wanted to my face.

She raised her voice petulantly. "Everybody on Horseshoe Park is so snobbish if you're not a regular here. I'll have to tag along with Jenny, just for company, and I hate it!"

Tiptoeing to the door, I slipped outside, easing the screen shut. I crossed our lawn to the white wooden lawn swing. Near the swing is a sign erected by the Horseshoe Park residents: PRIVATE. And below, on another board tacked to the same post: NO TRES-PASSING.

Clinging to the post, I gazed at the lake. *Oh no, you won't tag along with Jenny,* I thought. Tracy and I had a history of needing plenty of living space between us, and it had been my cousin who had started that tradition. Let it stay that way!

Unexpectedly I felt my hand grasped. I made a startled sound.

It was only Dawn. "Say that word, Jennifer."

I drew in a long breath. "*No trespassing.* It's a polite way of telling people who don't live here, *keep out.*"

chapter six

For supper we had sandwiches and chocolate milk
while Aunt Hertha bombarded us with plans. We'd
have dinners at noon, she announced, to get them over
with in the cool part of the day, and we'd eat off paper
plates: this would be an easy stay. She talked and talked,
but nobody really listened.

As soon as I finished eating I ran outside, anything
to get out of the cottage and away from Tracy. That
afternoon—just to steer clear of my cousin—I'd been
wandering around the Common, visiting all the houses,
friendlier than I'd been all summer.

It hit me suddenly how deserted the Horseshoe was
this evening. The long bench on the bluff over the lake
was empty. This was always the gathering place for the

33

kids at Loud, but it was getting so late in the season that no one was around.

I sat there looking down the board stairway that goes down to the lake. There are fifty-two steps to the T-pier from the bench on the bluff. Each summer I count, as if I expect the climb to grow easier.

It was dusk. No breeze. No waves. Nobody on the lake. It might have been a painted scene. Across the darkening blues and greens the gold of the setting sun was reflected in the east shore windows. Was it only yesterday that I'd been certain that this was going to be a golden two weeks.

Suddenly I heard footsteps behind me and when I turned around, there stood a tall young man about my age, with a fair, almost pale complexion. He looked more rumpled than the standard at Loud. "Hi," he said.

"Hello," I said. "Quiet, isn't it?"

"Yeah," he answered, moving pebbles around with his feet.

I studied his profile. All summer, Mr. Bjorkland had been teasing me about his handsome hippie grandson Todd, who was bumming his way east with some friends from college and would arrive at Loud, to sweep me off my feet, any minute. At the beginning of August Mr. Bjorkland had gone to join his wife in California, and Todd hadn't yet arrived. I'd forgotten all about him.

Well, he'd finally made it, and he certainly wasn't the

wild California type I'd expected from his grandfather's description. He seemed quiet and nice.

"Have you tried the water yet?" I asked him.

He looked at me curiously. "Isn't it cold after the sun goes down?"

"No." I laughed. "Except maybe by California standards."

He looked surprised when I mentioned California. Probably he didn't realize the closeness between the residents here, and how much we know about each other's families.

"See you later," I told him, getting to my feet. By the time I crossed the Common he was out of sight . . . but parked on the cottage steps was Tracy, watching.

My resentment boiled over. At that instant I decided to play a little game on my cousin. In the water of course, because she couldn't swim as well as I could.

Entering the cottage, I called, "I'm going for a swim, Aunt Hertha."

My aunt was in the living room, playing solitaire. "You aren't going swimming again." She drew a card from the deck she held in her hand and added it to the row on the table. "It's dark."

"I always take a dip at night."

"I don't want you going alone. Tracy, you go too."

That was what I wanted. I went through the kitchen to the back bedroom for my bathing suit. When I came out Tracy was wearing a white swimming suit that once was mine. With her long dark hair it was stunning. I started to compliment her, but I'd been brushed back so many times, I decided not to.

Aunt Hertha said, "Stick together, girls."

So that she wouldn't suspect I was planning anything, I began telling Tracy the gossip I'd heard that afternoon in visiting the cottages on the Common. "There are two houses empty. The Elemons next to us are traveling. Mrs. Bjorkland—she's next to Mrs. Cobb—is in California because a daughter is having another baby. I think I met one of her grandchildren today. At least he looked like a Bjorkland. There are so many I can't keep track. They visit Loud Lake in shifts."

"Is that the guy you were talking to on the bluff?" Tracy asked.

"Yes." I dove right in.

For a time I drifted close by, urging Tracy to plunge in, but she was reluctant. She'd decided she didn't want to get her hair wet.

Climbing out onto the diving board, I called, "One more good swim to the raft." Then I was underwater.

A few hard kicks and I was out of sight. I came up for air. Tracy was calling me. I didn't answer. Now when I went underwater I changed direction. I swam toward the far pier, which bordered the Horseshoe area on the east. It wasn't much distance for me. I wasn't even breathing heavily when I silently climbed out.

Tracy called again. Her voice had become shrill.

Crossing the Common, I sat down on the wooden swing by the NO TRESPASSING sign. I waited.

My cousin came fast. Half-running, half-stumbling, she made groaning sounds as her bare feet hit acorns.

"Hi," I said softly.

I could see her shadow against the background of sky and water. "Jenny?" she stammered in an unbelieving voice. She stood motionless.

I said casually, "I thought you were never coming."

My words touched her off. She was furious. "I think you're drowning, and all the time you're sitting up here laughing at me."

"It's just my way of saying, stop tailing me."

Her voice trembled. "Believe me, I'm not personally interested in anything you do. I'd rather be rid of you."

I slapped my legs before wrapping my damp towel around my shoulders to protect myself from the attacking mosquitoes. "Then, why?"

"Because my mother feels responsible for you."

"I'm in charge of me."

"That's what you think." Her voice rose with irritation. "It isn't fair. This was supposed to be *our* vacation. It makes me so mad the way we have to cater to your family."

Her bitterness astonished me. "What do you mean?"

"It's dull here for me. I don't know anyone but you. And here I am in your hand-me-down bathing suit. I get so sick and tired of your hand-me-downs! And all your clothes are beige, which just happens to be my worst color. But I've got to wear what you're tired of—even if the styles have changed."

I slumped over in the swing, filled with embarrassment. How strange to think that, for years, I'd felt virtuous about sending Tracy a dress that I really and truly wanted to hang onto for a while.

All the time my cousin had resented that—and me. Tonight she was letting me know it.

She caught hold of the swing's chain. "Then there's Dawn."

"Dawn?" Nonplussed, I said, "You aren't burdened with her an awful lot."

I heard her fist hit against the seat. "Are you kidding? I *live* with her. Always, always, Mom plans for her first. I may have to take care of Dawn all my life. Did you ever think about that?"

"But Dawn's sweet."

"That she is." She made an odd sound. "And even sweeter when you can be her tutor for one hour that's convenient for you. And then good-bye Dawn, until it's convenient again."

Her sarcasm bit through me. I shot out, "You just don't like me."

"You can't help what you are," she said and, actually, there was a hint of generosity in her voice.

"What am I?"

You'd think I'd yanked out the stopper of a bottle

labeled *Tracy Thane*. She poured out, "You make me scream. You act as if the world owes you the bright side of everything. Why are you so superior? You've never done anything for yourself—everything's been done for you."

She flung her arms about, and her hand collided with the sign beside the swing. She groaned, then exclaimed, "I never thought of it this way before, but you ought to wear this NO TRESPASSING sign around your neck. You're locked up safely, and there's no trespassing unless you give an invitation."

I'd avoided Tracy for years. Why hadn't it ever crossed my mind that she also was shunning me?

Her hot words continued. "I'll bet if you didn't get your way once you'd sit down and cry."

Years of frustration came out in one night's blast. She even brought Dan Mengers into the act! "You don't deserve him. You weren't serious about him until you saw other girls liked him. But then you figured he was worth having, and everything comes easy for you."

This was too much. "Shut up! You don't know anything about it!" I shouted, shaking with rage.

Fortunately, at that moment Aunt Hertha poked her head out of the cottage door. "There you are, girls. Come in now. Before I go to bed I want to hook our screens."

Tracy, too, must have been relieved to have our conversation brought to a halt, because she raced ahead, disappearing upstairs before the door slammed behind her.

How would we behave towards each other for two weeks in such close quarters?

I dreaded the morning.

chapter seven

During the night in that back bedroom I began stirring restlessly, vaguely conscious of some unusual noise. Generally Loud Lake is the opposite of its name —quiet. Half-awake, I pulled my pillow over my head.

Finally I sat up in bed.

It was a car horn. Somebody was either extremely persistent, or in trouble.

I put on my robe and slippers, and scuffed to the front porch. I heard other people on their porches. Here and there a flashlight slithered over the Common.

Now Aunt Hertha and Tracy appeared, dragging their robes around their shoulders, grumbling about being awakened.

"I guess a horn's stuck," I said.

Tracy yawned. "Let's go see."

We groped our way over the lawn in the direction of the noise. The horn seemed to be blaring at the rear of Mrs. Cobb's large clapboard house, and when Tracy and I arrived there at least a dozen people were fretting around an old jalopy. It was parked alongside the far end of Mrs. Cobb's privet hedge, almost hidden.

All that noise, and all those people, and nobody knew what to do. We could have saved someone from drowning, but how do you cope with a short circuit in a strange car?

We stood there in our nightclothes, feeling foolish. There's something more intimate about pajamas than the briefest of swimming suits. I don't imagine that dignified Mrs. Cobb ever dreamed that anything less than a fire or a tornado would propel her into a neighborhood conference with a mask of cream on her face and a net over her curlers.

Everybody talked. We jiggled the car. We twisted the driving wheel and pounded the horn button.

Suddenly Aunt Hertha appeared. "Call the police," she advised.

Mr. Laudman asked, "Whose car is it?"

No one seemed to know.

The horn wasn't losing strength. Aunt Hertha repeated, "Call the police."

At that moment, Todd Bjorkland came out of the dark. Without a word, he lifted the hood of the car. Even in the darkness he knew just where to put his hands.

Silence!

When the racket stopped we all shifted about uneasily, conscious of how weird we must look to each other. The Morrisons immediately vanished into the night. Young Kenny Laudman scurried back to his parents' cottage.

Only Mrs. Cobb seemed in no great hurry. She must have forgotten her appearance. Now that the emergency had been conquered she was as gracious in the middle of the night as if conversing with favorite customers at The Clearing. "Oh, you're Mrs. Bjorkland's grandson Todd. Let's see . . . if I remember, you haven't visited here at Loud Lake for at least five years. We heard you might be coming."

In the dark, the young man latched the hood of the jalopy. He's the quiet type, I wanted to tell Mrs. Cobb, who continued, "Well, it's good to have you here. I hope you'll stay a while. In fact, I've got a job for you. We need a strong fellow to take charge of the lawn-mowing. This summer there's only a crop of little fellows around."

Suddenly she must have remembered her appearance. She put her hands to her hair. "Well, we can talk about this tomorrow."

I was about to murmur a "good night" to the young stranger when I discovered he had vanished. I didn't hear him go. He said nothing, just dissolved. He must have been embarrassed by Mrs. Cobb's attention.

43

I looked around uneasily for Tracy. "Wait," I called to her drifting shadow. In the dark we stumbled over the roots of the oak trees.

"Hurry, girls," Aunt Hertha called from the cottage. "This has been a long day."

A long, long day. I listened to the squeaky floor overhead while my aunt and cousin got into bed. The first thing in the morning I'd ask to use the car.

I smiled ruefully. I was getting a dose of what Tracy claimed she had suffered through so long . . . I was learning what it was like to live at the convenience of relatives.

chapter eight

Even though my bedroom was next to the kitchen I slept right through breakfast. When I finally shuffled out, my aunt was the only person around. She had cleared a space on the table for her game of cards.

She put a black card on a red one before looking up at me. "We had waffles. There's batter left."

I shook my head. "I'll have toast and cranberry juice. Don't move."

"Dawn's been waiting for you."

"I promised her we'd walk to Loud for the morning paper." Leaning against the sink, I waited for my toast. "Where do you think we should have our lessons? It has to be a quiet place."

Aunt Hertha fanned her cards. "Poor child, she's so easily distracted. You've had lots of patience with her,

Jenny. I've told your mother time and again, I sure appreciate it."

"I have a special feeling for Dawn." Tracy's words of last night rankled. "Every time she hands me one of her letters I get a thrill."

"She knows she's different from other people. She's so lonely."

"I know." Taking a deep breath, I said, "After we walk to Loud, may I use your car?"

My aunt stopped moving the cards. Her eyes slid sidewise at me, and she chuckled. *"Already?"*

I carried my toast and juice to the table and sat on the edge of a chair. "In the rush yesterday I forgot my sewing box at home, and I want to work on the wool dress my mother and I cut out and fitted."

She grumbled, "You act like you've got nothing else to wear."

"I haven't. You sort of hurried me yesterday, and there are some odds and ends to take care of at home."

At that moment we heard Dawn's whistle outside, blown insistently. Springing up, I ran out and found her sitting in a tight ball on the white wooden swing, her legs drawn up under her to avoid the cold curious nose of Clinker, the Laudmans' black spaniel.

She was whimpering.

I said, "Look how his tail waves at you, sweetie. He wants to show you he's your friend."

Where was Tracy? She was supposed to be keeping

an eye on Dawn. My eyes scanned the Common, but nobody was visible except Mrs. Cobb with Todd Bjorkland, leaning over the electric mower, deep in conversation.

Dawn was whimpering again. I spun around to find her pressed into the corner of the seat, her eyes begging for help. Why was she trembling? Usually dogs didn't disturb her.

I pushed back her soft, dark hair from her wan face. It was then I saw the bluish mark on her wrist.

"What's this?" Turning over her arm, I saw that both sides were discolored. "Did you fall, sweetie?"

Her face began to work. She stared at me, one huge teardrop climbing to the lower lashes of each eye. Troubled as she was, she didn't know how to tell me about it.

A warm, protective surge of affection flooded through me. "Shall we walk to Loud now? We'll have a treat when I buy the newspaper," I told her, keeping my voice light. "Won't that be fun?"

She reached out to be lifted from the swing. I hugged her tense little body.

It's a beautiful hike to Loud. We walked along the path on top of the bluff overlooking the water. Most of the lots are landscaped all the way to the water's edge, and the gardens are lovely that time of year.

The usual fishy smell greeted us as we approached the tiny village, and music blared from the one dingy motel.

"It's dead," Dawn said.

She pointed at a small bloated fish, rising and falling where the waves lapped against the sand. Today she seemed to insist on sadness. She was not even indulging in her one-note singsong. Was she homesick? *Could* Dawn be homesick?

When we returned, Aunt Hertha had washed the dishes and swept the kitchen. She was really exasperated with Tracy for skipping out on the work. My cousin wasn't anywhere around, but Aunt Hertha was scolding her anyway.

After she'd taken Dawn upstairs for a nap, I said, "I have to go now, Aunt Hertha."

Although she was annoyed, I could see she was not as set against a trip to Rockwood as she had been when I first suggested it, so I rushed her before she could build up resistance. "I'll go now while there's no traffic. I'll be back by three. Is there anything I can do for you?"

"Well, you could water my plants."

"I'll take care of them." I reached for my sweater as if the matter were settled. I wouldn't give her an extra moment to think.

But Aunt Hertha made a clucking sound that caused my heart to sink. By this time I wanted to go so badly I could taste it.

"I'd rather you didn't go alone," she said.

The time had come to be honest. "I don't intend to be protected all the time. I won't be watched," I said. "I'm not used to being treated like a baby."

She ignored my outburst. "Where *is* Tracy? I haven't seen her for hours."

Together we searched. When we found my cousin she was squatting on the bottom of the fifty-two steps with Todd, shying small stones into the shallow water for Clinker to retrieve.

Todd nodded in recognition, but Tracy didn't look at me. "I don't want to drive to Rockwood. You go," she suggested to her mother. "I'll stay with Dawn."

Aunt Hertha seized on the idea. Immediately this became *her* trip. "Come on, Jenny," and she hurried across the lawn to the cottage. "Let's get started." Over her shoulder, she ordered, "Tracy, you'll have to stay in the house while Dawn has her nap."

Even now Tracy didn't turn around. "I'll come— when you go."

We'd traveled some miles before it occurred to me that my aunt was wearing a dress that was a discard of my mother's. The tweedy beige had been just right with my mother's chestnut hair, but it did not flatter Aunt Hertha's gray head in the slightest.

Impulsively I said, "Tracy's avoiding me. We had an argument last night."

Aunt Hertha turned to me. "Oh dear! Now what?" She smiled ruefully.

"She thinks I'm a do-gooder with Dawn. Aunt Hertha, Dawn's like my own sister. I'd do anything to help her."

49

Aunt Hertha drew back, and for a moment her chin seemed flattened against her neck. "I've always felt you and Dawn . . . in a way you're alike. Babes in the woods. Both of you are so trusting and vulnerable. Tracy's had to be a lot shrewder."

Her words astonished me. We drove some miles in a rare silence.

But Aunt Hertha couldn't stay speechless for long. "What would I do without your parents? Many's the night I can't sleep, and I look across the street, thankful I have them to depend on. I'd do anything for your father and mother."

I caught her eyes on me, looking at me with a curious hesitancy. "I say that—that I'd do anything for them— yet I don't like it much having to keep an eye on you while they're away. There's *such* a responsibility taking care of somebody else's child. For some reason, so much more so than your own. And then, as you know"—I saw how her hands tightened over the clasp of the safety belt she was wearing—"I'm stricter than your mother."

"I know."

"I put your parents on the spot, I guess. I should have told them sooner that I just couldn't go along with the idea of you alone in your house."

"They'd *promised.*"

"Don't blame your parents. They didn't change their mind until I changed it for them. I told them if I had to be responsible, I wanted you under *my* roof—and I knew I couldn't bring that about on Sawyer Street, so I just decided we'd go to the lake."

Her arms made one of their curling sweeps. "I was careful not to tell them *how* much earlier I planned we'd go to the lake. I figured when you exploded, I should be the one to take the blast."

She folded her hands, meekly—for Aunt Hertha. "I can stand up to Jenny, I told your mother. I'm not in a popularity contest as far as she's concerned. That's what I said."

It was a funny thing . . . my aunt was taking all the blame for upsetting my plans, yet I'd never liked her as much as I did now.

By this time we could see Rockwood in the distance. Changing the subject, my aunt began discussing Tracy's sixteenth birthday party, which was coming up next week.

All summer my cousin had been concentrating on that party, anticipating it the same way I'd been looking forward to staying alone while my parents were away.

My aunt sighed. "Imagine, Tracy's never had a big party in her life." What she didn't add was: you've had so many!

Her voice trailed off as we drove down quiet, decorous Sawyer Street with its sedate homes.

"How much time can I have?" I asked.

"Don't rush. I'll leave it up to you."

We parked in my aunt's driveway. Crossing Sawyer

51

Street, I surveyed our home with an eager, almost homesick feeling. The slate roofs of varying heights, the massive chimney at the front, and the timber designs on the stucco walls all spoke of strength to me. I saw the green of the lawn, a green that was amazingly vivid and alive in this month of August. The flowers were still in full bloom, but from somewhere near the hunchbacked oak came the autumn sound of a cicada.

With a catch in my breath, I unlocked the heavy front door. I pushed it open, and walked into the empty house.

chapter nine

The emptiness was alive, forbidding. I felt as if I'd been away an entire semester instead of one day. In the kitchen the faucet dripped so insistently I wanted to cry "Hush."

I wandered into the living room. Absently I picked up a pipe from the ashtray and propped it in my father's pipe stand. I walked out to the sun porch where Dawn and I had spent hours and hours, and back into the kitchen.

All of a sudden the emptiness closed in on me. Without my parents the place seemed huge and cold. I felt so alone! Automatically I reached for the phone to call Northcote's.

It was so noisy at the hardware store I could scarcely hear the girl who answered. "Dan's driving the delivery truck today," she said. She'd give him my message as soon as he came back. Lucky girl, I reflected, to see Dan all day at work.

I sat with my hand on the telephone, then decided that if I pretended to myself that I wasn't waiting, he'd return my call a lot sooner.

First I put my box of sewing material by the front door so that I wouldn't go off and forget it again.

En route to the kitchen, to clean up yesterday's dishes, I entered the dining room.

As I did I smothered a shriek.

In the window was a huge, jagged hole. And on the floor of the dining room was a rock.

It was a white, smooth rock about the size of a fist. It had the polished surface of those we'd picked up years ago on the Lake Michigan beach. My mother had put them in her rock garden. But this one was different. Grotesque.

It had been painted. Black eyes, a smudged nose, a large mouth with drooping corners, and then to top it, straw stuck on with gum . . . hideous! But the worst aspect was this: across the throat, someone had painted a gash of red nail polish.

Gingerly I picked it up to study it more closely.

Horrible!

I started to drop it when I saw a dirty scrap of paper stuck underneath. On it was scrawled, JUDGIE!!! HERES YOUR FAMILY PORTRAIT!!!

54

I closed my eyes but the rock didn't go away. It was there in all its repulsiveness when I looked again. The slashed throat seemed to glow.

This had smashed our window.

I shoved my fists against my mouth. My knees buckled under me. If only Mom and Dad were here, I thought wildly.

All of a sudden I stood up. There were too many hiding places in this large, rambling house.

I heard strange sounds—yes, positively—a door opening slowly, cautiously.

At that moment the floor in the front hallway squeaked.

I clapped my hand over my mouth to smother my frightened exclamation. Swinging about, I started to tiptoe hurriedly towards the kitchen. If I had time I could unbolt the back door. If not, I could circle through the back hallway, into the sun-room, the living room, and—I hoped—out the open front door.

I knew this house. That was my advantage—I thought.

But the intruder also knew this house. Too late I realized that he had not gone through the dining room, but had come directly from the front hall into the back hall and kitchen.

Jumping back, I shrieked—I'd bumped into him! My eyes almost popped out of my head, and I cried, "Dan!"

"You look at me as if—as if I were a werewolf."

"I expected you t—to phone," I gulped.

"I called in about a wrong address. When Midge told me you'd phoned, I drove right over." He stared at me, then asked abruptly, "What's wrong?"

Looking up at the face I knew by heart, I burst into tears. "Something terrible has happened."

I showed him the stone and the note. Even now, I looked away. The sight of it shattered me.

He hunched over to get a better look at the printed message. Finally he stood up. Dan has a square chin that juts when he is angry. It was jutting now. "Have you touched the stone?"

"I . . . I picked it up. Why?"

"It's evidence, Jenny."

"Evidence of what?"

"That's the law's business. But we ought not to smear it with fingerprints." Dan was tense and businesslike. "I wonder when this happened. Whoever threw it could easily—he might even be—"

Breaking off what he was about to say, his eyes surveyed the dining room and what he could see of the front hall. His face was a mask; but his manner was wary. "I think you'd better get out of here." He added grimly, "And you stay away from Sawyer Street!"

"But what shall I do—with th—that?"

"I'll take it to the police."

He asked for a newspaper to wrap it in. Never touching the stone with his fingers, he scooped it up with the dustpan and transferred it onto the paper. "Don't leave Loud Lake until you hear from me—*understand?*"

"What shall I tell Aunt Hertha?"

"Don't tell anybody anything," he said emphatically. "Let's leave everything to the police."

All of a sudden I remembered Eric Schallen. Quickly I told Dan what I'd read in the paper. "Oh, Dan—could he have done it?"

"I can't see why," Dan said thoughtfully. "He's probably on his way to Canada right now. Why would he bother with a prank like this? There are plenty of nuts in the world who would, though," he added.

I was ashamed of myself for crying, but I couldn't help it. "Oh Dan, if it hadn't been *you*. . . . If I'd been here alone, and found this th—thing. If it had been *him* sneaking—"

"Stop it, Jenny," he said fiercely.

Making his hand into a fist he bopped my chin. Then he stroked my cheek—and leaned over and kissed me.

chapter ten

So I returned to Loud Lake with better grace than before. I was glad to be out here where the ugly stone seemed remote and unbelievable.

I tried to put it out of my mind. Of course, I couldn't, not for an instant. Naturally, I would have liked to discuss it, but Dan had said no. It even would have been a relief to hear Tracy's opinion. I was beginning to feel differently about my cousin. She didn't know it yet—but then, she hadn't been brought up short by our conversation the way I had.

I wasn't really tempted to discuss the stone with Aunt Hertha because the threat would only result in a tighter surveillance on her part. If she already felt that the responsibility of her sister's child was a burden, just imagine how she'd react if she knew about the rock.

Dan had arranged for Northcotes' to replace the broken pane. We'd been so caught up in the events on Sawyer Street that day, that I'd forgotten to find out Dan's plans for the Harvest Festival, and whether he'd sold his car.

Wednesday. This was our first normal day at the lake and it set the pattern for all the days I'd have to stay here. After breakfast Aunt Hertha settled down with her cards, establishing herself on the porch in the midst of all activity. She talked to her cards. She enjoyed herself. It was fascinating; she could not be quiet without being noisy about it.

Nearby, I basted the sleeves into my new dress with Dawn seated beside me. She worked on a scrap of my wool with a snub-nosed scissors.

Nothing that happened on the Horseshoe escaped my aunt. "I'd never let *him* run a power mower of mine," she said, peering over her bifocals for a better look down the slope, where the noise of mowing was shattering the quiet. "You can tell he doesn't know the first thing about the machine he's riding."

Turning around, I saw that Mrs. Bjorkland's grandson was operating the riding mower while Kenny Laudman guided the lighter machine near the pathways and the trees. Aunt Hertha was right. Todd wasn't too good at the job. He left tufts of grass between the rows, but who cared in August? Just so he kept down the weeds and the quackgrass.

59

Watching, I tried to remember him as he'd been on his last visit here, five or six years ago. I wondered if I'd changed as much as he had. He seemed to have become so—I tried to think of the right word. Self-sufficient?

If he and Tracy could hit it off, it would be great. Yet though Tracy had been talking to him a lot, he seemed to seek *me* out.

I drew in a long breath. It would be so much easier if Dan were around. "Let's go for a walk, Dawn," I suggested, folding my material to take to Mrs. Cobb's later. "We've been sitting around all morning."

Dawn looked out at the mowing, at the children playing croquet, and at Clinker running wildly, trying to be part of everything that was going on.

"No," she said.

Since we'd come to Loud Lake it seemed to me that I saw secret worries hidden behind Dawn's beautiful, blank eyes, and she whimpered as she'd never done at home. I'd read a few books about retarded children, and though they seem to differ, one thing they have in common is a limited imagination. If Dawn was frightened, it was because something actually had scared her.

"Shall we go in the boat? Shall we make waves?"

She shook her head. The heart-shaped face was shadowed.

Aunt Hertha whispered, "Give her time."

I went into the bedroom and put on my swimming suit. When I came out onto the porch, Dawn pressed

60

herself into the corner behind the table where her mother was playing cards. Protecting herself from having to go near the water. What a shame!

"After I swim, will you go to Mrs. Cobb's house and help me sew?"

She nodded jerkily.

Circling the Common, I walked close to the cottages to avoid the mowers. When I came to the stairway on the bluff, something made me turn and search out the lonely, wan face pressed against the screen of our yellow house.

My heart turned over. Why was she so fearful?

Perhaps she'll write me another letter, I planned. Maybe something will slip out in writing that she can't talk about.

Slowly I walked down to the pier. The steps were hot under my bare feet.

There was Tracy on the pier, stretched out flat, eyes closed, chin elevated, straps pushed off her shoulders, oiled and baking. She must have heard me come, but she didn't look up.

Parking my beach towel and lotion, I sat dangling my legs. "You're pink," I said finally. "Turn over. I'll oil your back."

She made sort of a grunting sound. Opening her eyes, she squinted at me. "Oh—it's you."

I shriveled inside at the tone of her voice. But I knew nothing could be gained by keeping our conversation on

61

tiptoes, so I trod heavily. "Tracy, let's be friends. If we aren't, it'll be too uncomfortable for everybody."

"I don't mind being uncomfortable, but I don't want my mother on my neck." She was opening the way for a truce.

The sun was beautifully warm. There was a dream quality about the water which seemed to meet the sky in the southern bay. In the distance the boats sailed from the water right through the sky. Above us, out of view on the bluff, we could hear children playing on the Common. The loud mowing had ceased, and when I glanced up I saw Todd resting on the long bench, watching us.

Tracy's voice interrupted my musing. "I wish he'd come down and talk to us."

"He's kind of shy. I think he has to be invited."

"Maybe he'll come now that you're here," Tracy said, letting her resentment show.

I didn't want to get into another disagreement, so I changed the subject. "Tracy, your mother was talking to me about your party next week. I've been thinking . . . when the two of you drive back to Rockwood for the party, I can take care of Dawn out here."

Utter silence.

Then, jerking to her elbow, Tracy flung back her lovely dark hair. For the first time today she looked at me full face. "I'd like that. With Dawn out here at the lake it won't matter how noisy we are at home." She paused. "It isn't that I'm ashamed of my sister," she said stoutly.

"I know, Tracy," I said quickly. "She does get over-excited."

Now that we were on the subject of her party, Tracy was dying to talk about it. Flinging her arms about exuberantly, she redecorated the house for my benefit. She worked hard at the description, and gloried in the accomplishment. And she even thanked me for offering to keep Dawn.

As decreed by Aunt Hertha, at noon we ate a huge meal of baked potatoes and pork chops and a green-bean casserole so that we could coast through the rest of the day without heating the kitchen.

But Dawn wouldn't eat, and I was really worried. During lunch my mind searched about for something that would catch her interest. In the fastness of her thoughts no one could reach her. She was troubled.

Tracy, though, was radiant. Her chattering made me think of my own June birthdays, all of them spent here at the cottage.

"Tracy!" I burst out impulsively. "Cancel the order for your birthday cake. Let me make you a fortune cake."

She looked receptive, but uncertain. "A fortune cake?"

In the cottage someplace there was a collection of

63

small charms, each with a special meaning. My mother kept them at the cottage because all three of us have summer birthdays. "The charms are metal, and you bake them right in the cake. Whatever you find in your particular piece of birthday cake tells your fortune."

In simple words I explained this to Dawn. "We always say, *chew carefully.*"

"Chew . . . carefully," she repeated.

Tracy liked my offer. "A fortune cake! That really sounds fun. Can we look at the tokens, Jenny?"

Standing on a chair, I searched the top kitchen shelf. There were leftover candles and the paper sack containing the fortune charms.

I poured them onto the table. "Look, sweetie. Aren't they cute?"

Dawn fingered a tiny teapot.

"That means hospitality," and I tried to explain in simple words what hospitality meant, but it was too much for her. She looked blank.

"The heart," I said, "that's love. I love you, sweetie," and leaning over, I kissed the tip of her nose. There was so much Dawn could never be, but she *was* a loving little girl.

Oddly endearing in her excitement, Tracy spilled over. "What a great idea, Jenny! What does the coin mean?"

"Good fortune. There's a list someplace, explaining all of them. It's probably in the desk under the stairway. We'll look."

*　　　*　　　*

After we'd eaten, I decided to have a quiet session with Dawn. She needed routine now that she had been thrown into a life completely strange to her.

I set up a card table in the living room, rather than the porch, because I didn't want any distractions. I'd found I even had to use plain material rather than a patterned cover on what we called our *desk*. I mustn't wear jingly bracelets. I had to use one-word commands.

Oh, I could lose Dawn so quickly.

She sat on the edge of a chair that wasn't quite the right size, but it was the best we had in the cottage. Her large eyes clung to my face. It was the trust there that got me.

"Good afternoon, Dawn."

"Good afternoon, Jennifer."

Today we would talk about color. What is color? You can't smell it; you can't taste it; you can't hear it; you can't feel it. You can see a color. What is yellow? The sun. Bananas. Corn on the cob. At Loud Lake Dawn had seen many yellows. What is blue? Blueberries. The sky. Sometimes the lake. And red, what is red?

She looked up at the ceiling, down in her lap, then said in a flat voice, "The stone."

I looked at her, appalled. "*What* stone?"

I had an insane impulse to seize my little cousin, to shake information from her. But that was all she would say and, unintentionally, I must have pressed her too hard, because over her face came the expression that preceded a storm.

I sat, staring, shivering a little.

"Are you tired?" I asked, after a little while.

It wasn't a good session, though we both worked hard at it. Dawn seemed absorbed. Then I became conscious of the monotonous one-note humming. Unhappy little girl!

"Sweetie," I said, quite at the end of my invention. "Let's go to Mrs. Cobb's. At least I'll get something done, and you can watch the lake. Okay?"

She nodded.

Mrs. Cobb welcomed us. She had set up her machine on the glassed porch overlooking the lake. The porch was filled with Oriental mementos from the days when she and her husband traveled, and with house plants creeping from the window ledges onto all the tables and shelves in the room.

She was on her way to work at The Clearing. "Stay as long as you like," she said, "but latch the back door when you leave." She put her hand to her brow. "I just remembered—Todd wants to be paid every day. He says he never knows when the urge to go will come to him." She stood by the window scanning the lakefront. "I can't see him." She pulled a bill from her purse. "Will you give him this?"

I went to the window and put the money in my

pocket. "Sure. Oh there he is, talking to Tracy on the long bench."

Mrs. Cobb looked curious, but she was in too much of a hurry to pursue him.

I watched them for a minute, because it was fascinating to try to figure out what Tracy's wildly waving arms could mean. When they went their separate ways, Tracy's wave was a great flourish while Todd's was a restrained salute. I sighed. They hadn't been talking for more than two minutes: I wasn't a very good matchmaker, I decided.

Alone with Dawn, I started sewing. "Would you like to write me a letter?" I suggested to her as she wandered about restlessly. "Tell me about your trip to Loud Lake."

She didn't answer. When I looked around I saw she was staring out the window. Her dark brows were drawn together, and although she wasn't whimpering aloud I knew she was whimpering inside.

"Dawn." I saw the nervous quickness with which she lifted her head.

"Let's go to our cottage and have a treat," and folding my sewing across my arm, I picked up the money. We stopped at the Bjorklands', but there was no answer, and I didn't see Todd on the Common. Well, I could give him his pay later.

I wondered what we'd do when we got back to the cottage. With both Tracy and Aunt Hertha on the beach, I'd have to keep this tired little girl occupied. I was beginning to realize what a drain her constant need for supervision must be for them.

As Dawn and I entered the empty cottage, I heard the sound of rushing water. When I went into the kitchen to check the faucet, the room was a mess. The shelf doors were ajar, the oven was open, and there were crumbs on the counter. Tracy considered it cleaning up the kitchen if she washed a few dishes. She hadn't even put the food away.

But the water wasn't running. I turned the faucet on absentmindedly. The trickle didn't make much noise. It wasn't what I'd heard.

Then suddenly I *knew.*

It had been the sound of the toilet being flushed. I went to look, but the float wasn't stuck, and the tank was full.

I felt baffled—even afraid. "Something's wrong here, or else I'm going crazy," I exploded to Dawn.

She looked up at me. Two small tears glistened in her large eyes.

chapter eleven

"Dear Cousin, It is a hot day. The wind blows hot. The bench is hot. The steps is hot.

"Loud Lake is big. It has waves and fish. A dog swims. Shut up. It barks. It is black. Shut up. A man mows. Like on Sawyer Street. Shut up. I stay in the cottage.

"Tracy has got a birthday. Jennifer will bake a cake. It will show 16 candles. Mommy and Tracy had a fight. Shut up. It was for a can of beans. Shut up.

"Because my letter is getting long I will close.

"Your cousin, Dawn Thane."

Friday noon. Lying on the pier, I studied the letter Dawn had handed me when I left the cottage. Her big eyes had clung to my chin as if she were afraid to lift them higher. Her fingers had clutched the screen door.

I could tell she'd put all she was capable of into this letter—how she'd tried! All morning she'd hung over the kitchen table with her legs twisted around the chair, small beads of perspiration clinging to her upper lip. And now she could hardly wait . . . would she get a blue star? A gold one?

Today the pier was jammed. The Laudmans were entertaining at an annual family picnic and Kenny was showing off to a crowd of relatives.

To avoid them I was lying along the extreme eastern bar of the T-pier. Again I studied Dawn's letter. I was baffled. *Shut up, shut up.* Where had that come from? Had I heard anybody around here using those words? No, not even Tracy and Aunt Hertha last night when they'd squabbled over the baked beans that Tracy had left on the grocery counter, after she'd paid for them.

Dawn had written about the lake. She had written about Clinker. *I stay in the cottage.* Did that mean more than it said?

Suddenly I jumped. Tracy was dripping water on my back. Sitting down beside me, she touched her toes in the water.

My eyes rounded; then I whistled. She was wearing a new red-and-white bikini.

"Like it?" she purred. "I talked Mom into it yesterday." She and Aunt Hertha had gone to the grocery store and the laundromat with Mrs. Cobb. "It's cheap, but I like the style."

"With that on your mind, no wonder you forgot the baked beans," I teased.

"But I didn't, Jenny." Her hands stabbed the air around us. "That's the crazy thing. I put the beans on the shelf right above the stove. I remember it."

"Okay," I said softly. She didn't need me to pick on her, too.

We lay there while a strong hot wind bent the long grasses on the bluff where it was too steep for mowing. It turned the trees into tossing plumes. Really, it was not a comfortable day. The boathouse door slammed. The bottoms of the small boats moored alongside the pier slapped . . . slapped. . . .

I had to snatch for my towel and weigh it down with my sandals. "It's getting choppy out there."

Tracy pulled herself up beside me. "There's a tornado alert on the weather reports." She shook water from her long hair like a dog. "Should the water-skiers be out there?"

"They love this kind of water. It's okay — they wear life jackets."

"There's Todd up on the bluff." She waved to him to join us.

Todd came down the fifty-two steps to the pier. "I have a message for you."

"Message? For me?" I said doubtfully.

"Your friend Dan Mengers telephoned from Rockwood. Mrs. Cobb had to go to work, so she asked me to tell you." Mrs. Cobb has the only telephone, and she's awfully nice about running an answering service for the rest of us.

"He'd like you to meet him at the Big Hollow Festival Sunday instead of on Labor day," Todd went on. "You should phone him if you can't be at the Old Records stall at noon."

A day earlier with Dan! Suddenly I felt light-headed and impulsively I blurted, "Wouldn't you like to go to the Festival with us, Todd? It must be sort of dull for you at the lake."

He hesitated. He seemed all arms and legs, and bones and angles. Did he eat enough, bumming around on his own?

"It'll be just the four of us," Tracy added.

"Well, if I'm around this weekend," he said. "It would be fun."

I was really pleased. He could be an audience for Tracy, giving Dan and me privacy. We had so much to talk about. "I hope you can come," I said earnestly.

He smiled in reply. In his hand was a piece of driftwood that he'd been whittling, and for a few minutes he sat with us on the pier, his pocket knife working away at it.

"I bet he doesn't come," Tracy muttered, as we walked home.

"What do you mean?"

"Now that he knows you're not available, he's not going to tag along with me."

72

"He's not interested in me," I protested. "You're the one he talks to."

"I'm the one who talks to *him*," Tracy corrected me.

"Well, he's the quiet type. He doesn't talk much to anybody."

She was unconvinced. "You know what I talk about that he finds so interesting?"

I shook my head.

"You."

And she ran on ahead of me towards the cottage.

chapter twelve

Saturday night Tracy and I made cucumber sandwiches for supper. It was my aunt's idea: the hot weather had gotten to her. It was above ninety and humid. The worst part was that the heat settled in the cottage, making the nights as breathless as the days. Aunt Hertha complained that even shuffling her cards was work.

She listened to the weather reports. "Tornado weather," and she planned what we'd do in this cottage with no basement if a black funnel cloud poured this way. There was a new plan for each weather report. I got mixed up. The latest: we'd crouch in the culvert in back of the Morrisons' cottage.

A sweet excitement swept through me when I thought about seeing Dan. "At the Festival," I said to Tracy, "if you should happen to get lost—"

Tracy smiled. "I read you loud and clear."

"Take Todd with you." Despite her remarks the other night, she was really looking forward to the day with Todd.

I caught the gleam of her grin. "I'll do my best. I feel as if I've had a great triumph—getting him to swim with me today. Wouldn't you think somebody coming from California would be expert in the water? But then, I suppose, not *everybody* lives on the Pacific. It just seems that way."

My mind had wandered back to its chief topic of interest. "I wonder why Dan is meeting me there instead of calling for me?"

"He's probably hitching a ride."

If Todd was there to occupy Tracy, I'd have a chance to tell Dan what Dawn had said about the red stone. It haunted me. There seemed to be no way of getting more information from her. Certainly, I'd tried.

Sunday morning Tracy and I tanned ourselves out on the raft. We were quite gay while we dressed for the Festival and waited for Todd.

An hour later he hadn't shown up.

"Jilted," Tracy said, shrugging.

"Well, he said he might not make it," I offered weakly. I was as disappointed as she was.

Waving good-bye to Dawn and Aunt Hertha, we started off without him.

I turned to Tracy. "Instead of the highway let's go by Lake Williams, and avoid the traffic. Okay?"

"You're the driver."

We drove through fields of tasseled corn with here and there a pasture where cattle grazed. The narrow road had sharp-angled corners, dips and rises, but no billboards—just an occasional slogan about chewing tobacco painted on the side of a barn. With the windows down, the hot air funneled through the car, battering my damp hair. My lips were parched. Ahead on the asphalt the heat shimmered in waves.

As we drove, I saw a wedge of geese flying across the sky above us, a sure sign of colder days ahead.

I nudged Tracy. She helped me watch them out of sight.

"This'll be my last free summer," she said. "When I'm sixteen I'll have to work. I can't squander the summer the way you do."

I winced, but then I realized she was simply stating a fact of life. She wasn't trying to put me down.

"No more baby-sitting or clipping hedges," she said. "I'm going to job-hunt early so I won't have to take just anything." She told me about a friend of hers who worked in an automatic car wash, gesturing wildly as she described wiping off the windows and chrome of automobile after automobile.

A smile flickered on her lips. "Maybe I'll be a nurse's aide—with my own paycheck."

Just then the car engine stopped.

"No gas," said Tracy, disgusted.

"Impossible!" I guided the car onto the shoulder of the road and looked at the gauge incredulously. The indicator was stuck on *E*. "But yesterday I had it filled in Loud and drove right back to the cottage."

"So what do we do now?"

I groaned. "No gas stations for miles on this road." I slumped over the wheel. "Dan'll think we're not coming."

"That's all you think about—Dan."

"Not *all*. I'm thinking about how infuriating this is, and I'm thinking about the money for more gas."

"Do you think we have a leak?"

I was about to hop out of the car to have a look, although what good that would do I didn't know, when a farmer came down the road on a tractor.

He shut off his noisy machine. "Trouble?"

"Out of gas," I said helplessly. "How far is the nearest station?"

"Too far. Wait here," he said, as if we could do anything else. "I'll fetch you a gallon of gasoline from my barn." That would be enough to take us to Slade's Corner, where we'd find a filling station.

The car was a furnace in the hot sun. It must have been 120 degrees. There were no trees, no shade. "I can't breathe," Tracy said.

"Let's roll under the fence and sit in the cornfield until he gets back."

We crouched in the dust. I groaned. "I'll be a mess when we meet Dan."

She stuck her chin around a cornstalk. "There you go again. *Dan.*"

At that moment we heard the noise of another car approaching. I hoped the driver would realize that my car, which was partly blocking the road, was stopped.

He slowed down, and simultaneously Tracy and I gasped. The other car was the jalopy with the short in the horn from Horseshoe Park. The driver, Todd Bjork-land.

He glanced at our car and drove on.

Tracy's face brightened visibly. "Oh, Jenny," she crowed. "He's going to meet us! He decided to come after all! I wish that farmer would hurry up. I hope Todd can find us in those crowds!"

It was good to see Tracy so pleased, but I was almost certain Todd had no idea how difficult it would be to find us in the mob that gathered for the Festival.

"Tracy," I interrupted, tugging at her arm. "He didn't recognize our car. Doesn't that strike you as odd?"

"Oh, don't be silly," she answered impatiently. "Do you know how many blue Fords there are in the world?"

Just then the tractor chugged into sight. I slapped dust from my dress, and stamped it off my sandals.

We paid the farmer and thanked him for his trouble. It wasn't far to Slade's Corner. We were lucky. We wouldn't be late at the Old Records stall.

Maybe we wouldn't find Todd, but at least I'd get to see Dan.

chapter thirteen

For fifteen years the Big Hollow Harvest Festival had been gaining in popularity as *the* place to be on Labor Day weekend—but it was getting out of hand, I thought crossly. Population explosion, wow! The smell of frying onions and broiling hamburgers assailed us, mingling with barnyard odors of the trading posts where people were selling rabbits and kittens and chickens and goats. Tracy and I were carried along Swapper's Lane to the Old Records stall by a tidal wave of humanity.

Dan is so tall that he stands out in a crowd. But it was not until we wove our way into touching distance that we saw there was someone with him. There was no sense in hoping it was Todd, for they had never set eyes on each other. Tracy was convinced it was, though, and the disappointment registered on her face when she saw it was Jim Northcote.

My eyes met Tracy's. We both breathed a sigh.

Jim is stocky and pink-cheeked. Even standing still he seems to be in motion, jingling loose things in his pockets or hunching his shoulders in various directions.

"The boss's son," Dan said. "Tracy, you know Jim?"

"I know Amy Wilkins," Tracy said.

Jim grinned at the mention of his vacationing girl friend, not catching the bitterness in Tracy's voice. Oh, I felt for her. I hoped Todd would find us.

"We're dehydrated," I said to Dan.

"That's my girl. Always begging." He explained about the change in plans. "I sold the car. Then I was stranded because my parents went off for the weekend. I had to bum a ride with Jim, and he could only come today."

We ambled about. Two hours later we were still looking for something to drink, but the stands were so crowded now that it seemed easier to stay thirsty. I tried to keep us a group so Tracy wouldn't feel she was being forced on Jim, but that became too much of a struggle.

We arranged a meeting spot. I felt sorry for Tracy, but now Dan and I could really talk.

Right away, I told him what had happened during my session with Dawn. "We were having a lesson on color. Red, she said—*like on the stone.*"

I heard Dan gasp. "What else did she say?" Hot as

81

it was, Dan put an arm around my shoulder. I felt cherished and protected. "What did she say about the stone?"

"You know Dawn. A door opens, a few words slip out, the door closes. And I mean, it closes."

We drifted on. Presently we came to a hamburger stand that wasn't too crowded. Dan bought two hamburgers for each of us and we carried them to an open field in back of the tents. I welcomed the sight of the billowing, tumbling clouds in the sky: we might have a break in the heat.

"Have the police told you anything about the stone?" I asked.

Dan grinned. "They don't consult with me."

I don't know how long we sat there, chatting, surmising, doing what Dan called "a Perry Mason." Time simply dissolves when I'm with him.

But we couldn't figure out how Dawn could have seen the horrible stone with the red nail polish on it. We couldn't even decide if that was the stone she meant. Maybe she had seen a red stone, like a ruby, in someone's jewelry. But where? And when? We finally gave up.

Dan turned his head to listen as a portable radio went by. "It's raining in Chicago."

I glanced upward. "And coming this way."

Dismayed, I realized our day together would have to be cut short. He steered me towards the big beer sign where we were supposed to meet Tracy and Jim. We had to wait for them. People were scurrying around, tying down tent flaps, and bracing against the squall.

Finally Tracy and Jim came into sight. "Oh, my mother will be worried sick with these high winds," Tracy said. "We've got to hurry back to the lake. Where's the car?"

Good question. I'd forgotten. We searched and searched.

When we finally found the car, Dan shoved me in and shut the door, then stood in the busy traffic directing me so I could drive onto the highway. We didn't even get to say good-bye. "Be careful," he shouted, and was gone.

I tried to sort out my impressions of the day. I felt shortchanged, but not half as cheated as my cousin. I wondered if Todd was still looking for us at the fairgrounds. I scarcely failed to notice that Tracy was silent, too. The long breath which exploded from between her lips as we coasted through Loud drew me back.

"We made it," she said in a relieved voice. "I knew you didn't have much money, and I sure don't have any."

"For what?"

"Didn't you *know?*" Leaning forward she tapped the gas indicator. It hovered near *E.*

I could actually feel my mouth drop open. "Crazy!"

"Crazy," Tracy agreed.

chapter fourteen

Labor Day morning. I was sitting in the wooden swing with Dawn when a strange car swung into our parking space, ignoring the NO TRESPASSING sign.

It was a strange car, yes, but Dan was driving it! "Dan!" I shouted, in what sounded like somebody else's voice, I was so surprised. His unexpected arrival confused me, and I was embarrassed at my appearance. My hair . . . this old swimming suit.

He gave me a strange look before he turned to Dawn with a gentle, formal greeting while they shook hands. My young cousin likes to shake hands.

"Well," I laughed, "couldn't you have given me a hint yesterday?"

"It's a surprise to me too. Believe it or not, the police loaned me this car. I'm to invite you for a ride in it."

84

I felt a quick little stirring of alarm. "What's happened, Dan?"

"They found the doors of your house open this morning. It looks like an act of sheer defiance, because nothing was disturbed."

"Nothing stolen?"

"They don't think so," Dan said. "But of course, the police don't know the place. They want you to check. At first, they asked me to come up here with them, to show them the way. But with the Labor Day parade they're so shorthanded that they took me up on it when I offered to get you myself." Abruptly he looked around. "Where's your aunt? Are you alone?"

I nodded. "When she heard Tracy and me discussing everything we'd seen at the Festival yesterday, she decided she had to see for herself. And since Tracy isn't much interested in staying here now that Todd seems to have left, she went along. Dawn and I are taking care of each other."

He put his hand on Dawn's head. "I'm taking you for a ride, Dawn."

I dressed her quickly and then threw on an old dress. I didn't bother to leave a note for my aunt because we'd be back long before she was.

There was a patrol car parked in front when we arrived at the house. Dan swung Dawn onto his shoulder, and she giggled with pure delight as he went up the walk.

85

A patrolman not much older than we were was waiting for us. He accompanied me from room to room. Nothing seemed disturbed. I counted the silver service. I found my mother's fur jacket. Although there were gaps in her jewelry, that was understandable. She had taken some of her best things with her, and I remembered her saying she would put her few antique pieces in the bank vault.

I looked in drawers and closets. As far as I could see, nothing had been touched.

"How about televisions, stereos, appliances—things that are easily disposable?" the policeman asked.

"All present and accounted for."

"Did your father have any guns?"

I shook my head. "He fishes."

We went from basement to attic; nothing was disturbed.

We were about to leave when I noticed that a small framed snapshot of my father and myself, taken at Loud Lake last summer and a favorite of my mother's, had fallen on its face on the fireplace mantel.

"Just a minute," I said, and reached to stand it up.

The frame was empty. The photo was gone.

That was odd. Had my father decided to take it to show to our relatives in Sweden? No, I would have noticed.

I don't know what made me glance into the fireplace. The next minute I gasped. There was the snapshot.

It had been ripped in half and dropped onto the brick floor inside the protective screen. In the entire house that was the only thing different today . . . the snapshot with the jagged tear that beheaded my father and me.

When Dan took me back to Loud Lake he wouldn't leave me there alone with Dawn. He insisted he was staying until my aunt came and, believe me, I was glad.

We loitered on the pier while the other residents who marked Labor Day as the end of the season put their cottages in order for the winter. Of course, there'd be October weekends ahead when the water pipes would be drained, but today the refrigerators would be pretty well cleaned out; the mothballs would be scattered in blankets.

The events of the day still obsessed me, even in the tranquility of the deserted pier.

"In real life," I admitted to Dan, "I don't like mystery."

The police had taken the torn snapshot for fingerprints. "Although if it's the same person who threw the stone there won't be fingerprints. We're not dealing with an amateur in this case," the officer had said.

This time the police told me not to visit Rockwood until my parents returned. *As if I would!*

Dan lay on the pier and studied the sky. "Are you going to tell your aunt?"

"I'll just say I went into Rockwood with you."

87

When my aunt and Tracy drove up, they were too excited about their bargains to be more than mildly curious about my news. They weren't surprised to see Dan. They never noticed the car he was driving. And Dan, feeling he ought to return it as soon as possible, left right away.

The Common was deserted that night when Dawn and I went to the bluff to sit on the backless bench. The cottages were locked up earlier than on most weekends.

The moon was cold-white and bright. I put my arm around Dawn's shoulder and hugged her close. Autumn sadness pricked through me. Not only was Labor Day cutting off summer, but this year it was leaving my childhood behind. A whole new life lay ahead at the university. Nostalgia for all the summers at Lake Loud overwhelmed me.

I sighed. If only Dan and I were going to the same college!

Dawn whispered, "It's dark, Jennifer."

"That's because a cloud is passing in front of the moon." I tried to divert her. "Tell me, what did you do yesterday when I was at the Festival?"

"We talked to the lady."

"What did you talk about with Mrs. Cobb?"

"She lost one too."

"One what?" I asked.

"A can," she said. "With salmon in it."

Here we were, back to the missing can of beans. I picked her up, to reassure her.

"It got lost." She was running her whistle back and forth on the chain around her neck. "It was the lady's salmon."

"I'm sure she's got more." I stretched my sweater around both of us and buttoned us in together. She liked that. I could hear her breathing, almost purring.

Except for our solitary porch light where Aunt Hertha was playing cards, everything was dark. How did Mrs. Cobb endure it here when the summer residents left? This was my first experience at not departing on Labor Day. I didn't like it.

Suddenly a branch cracked behind me. I jumped a little, and Tracy came out of the dark. "What gloom! Has everybody gone except us?"

As if in answer, Mrs. Cobb's car swept around the rear of the cottages and she came over to chat. Aunt Hertha, hearing us across the deserted Common, hurried through the dark to join us.

During the past week she and Mrs. Cobb had become chummy. Their conversation now naturally drifted to Tracy's birthday party, for Mrs. Cobb had offered to drive to Rockwood to deliver the cake I was going to bake.

"Mrs. Cobb, it's just wonderful of you to offer to bring Tracy's birthday cake in," and Aunt Hertha thanked her again.

"I think it's wonderful of Tracy to be having her sixteenth birthday, and wonderful of Jenny to bake the cake," said Mrs. Cobb, laughing.

Aunt Hertha and Tracy planned to leave Thursday for Rockwood. They'd do the shopping for her party that afternoon. Dawn and I would stay here, and I'd bake the fortune cake. Friday morning, before she went to work, Mrs. Cobb would deliver the cake.

Tracy sighed. "It's great to be able to give a party like this at the beginning of school. I'll be set for the year."

Mrs. Cobb drew her sweater over her shoulders. "I'd hoped to have the park mowed again before autumn. But Todd was a most independent young man." She laughed, but I could tell by the tightness in her voice that she was forcing herself to be charitable. "I guess he wasn't very happy at Loud Lake."

Tracy was standing on the bluff's edge, shying stones into the water below. We could hear the *plunk,* and the wash of the waves slapping the shore. The boats were creaking and rattling. Above us clouds lashed through the sky and the moon was a spotlight, on and off.

Tracy said, "Jenny, what are those bright things flashing in the water?"

I went to the head of the steps. "Where?"

"Over there, near where the Laudmans tie their boat."

Mrs. Cobb fretted, so Tracy and I went down to look. What she had seen turned out to be discarded garbage; the shining objects were tin cans.

Mrs. Cobb was really upset. Nothing like this had ever happened here before! "My blood pressure!" she complained.

90

When Tracy and I cleaned up what we could find in the dark, we discovered that the cans had contained baked beans and salmon. We dumped the cans in an old bait pail. We didn't say much, but I felt our minds were traveling along the same puzzling pathway.

From out of nowhere the thought of the NO TRESPASSING sign flashed through my mind. "When people like my parents and Mrs. Cobb say things aren't like they used to be, I've always shrugged it off," I mused. "But you know, this wouldn't have happened a few years ago."

Tracy sighed. "All my life, coming to Loud—even on your family's charity—has been a big treat. But this time it's been one unpleasant thing after another. Tonight, it almost seems sinister here."

And as I looked up at the deserted bluff in the twilight, I had to agree.

chapter fifteen

Bleak. That's the only word to describe the day after Labor Day. The waves tumbled in a leaden lake. Not a boat was visible.

My aunt had the radio turned on loud. She was listening to a tornado alert. While she and Tracy talked above the radio, I sat with my head propped in my hand, dawdling with my toast and syrup as I never would have at home.

Suddenly I heard Dawn in the other room, shouting, "Shut up, shut up." When I hurried into the living room I found her clutching her favorite doll by its wrist. She was shaking it violently.

I had to force open Dawn's rigid fingers. "Sweetie, she's been a good girl."

She wouldn't talk to me. She bowed her head, and picked at her fingers. But she wouldn't speak.

We're all on edge, I thought.

Was it the weather? Was it the letdown after Labor Day? Were these things getting to my young cousin too, or did she imitate the moods of adults? "Let's walk to Loud," I suggested.

"There's quite a wind. Wrap her up well," Aunt Hertha called from the kitchen.

The walk was a mistake. It was far brisker along the lake than I had expected, and I urged Dawn to hurry. She scuffed along silently.

When we finally reached the village the store was closed. We crossed the street to the tiny post office. "Can I get a morning paper?" I asked elderly Mr. Beech.

He shook his head. Peering over his bifocals, which sat below the hump on his large nose, he studied Dawn. "She has a duck-legged walk," he said, not unkindly. "I've knowed them that was slow to learn, but once they catch on to anything they don't forget it."

By now the wind was gusting up to fifty miles an hour. Although I tried to shield Dawn, the wind swept her breath away, and she clutched my hand tightly.

Across the Common I could see Aunt Hertha standing at the door, a worried expression on her face. "I thought you'd never come. I've been watching the sky. It's bad!"

I looked up. Clouds swirled crazily across the heavens. "There's no funnel," I breathed.

"Not yet," she said, her voice full of foreboding.

The trees were writhing as if they were in pain. Dust was flung in the air. Presently the western sky became an ominous blue-black, and swift stabs of lightning struck fear in my heart. Thunder began—far off at first, then on every side, loud, in great rolling cadences.

Rain. There were no warning drops, just tubs of water in solid sheets. The Common soon had rivers and pools I'd never seen there before.

Then hail. We could hear it smashing down on the roof.

Dawn pressed her face against my sweater. "It's all right, it's all right," I whispered to comfort her.

Tracy stood at a west window, gasping at the tumult. I heard Aunt Hertha suck in her breath, then muffle a cry when the huge branch on one of the old oaks cracked off with an explosive sound.

I wished I were home in our solid old house. This cottage seemed so frail. How could it stand up to such buffeting?

Presently the wind made a high-pitched whistle. While I watched the devil's dance in the treetops I noticed Mrs. Cobb standing on her porch, waving what looked like a huge beach towel.

"She's signaling," Tracy said, over my shoulder.

"If it lets up at all we'll dash down there," Aunt Hertha said, on a tremulous breath. "Her house is stronger than this even if it's on the bluff, and she's got a basement."

I stared at my aunt. "You'd go out in this?"

"If we get wet we won't shrink. But the hail—" She placed a sheltering hand on Dawn's head. "We'll stick it out here just a bit longer." Her voice trailed off forlornly.

Now the lights blinked, then went off. How awesome. No radio. No hum in the refrigerator.

"No hot lunch unless we can make it to Mrs. Cobb's," said Aunt Hertha, who kept meals uppermost in her mind no matter what came up. "She's got gas."

Suddenly I had an idea. "The car is next to the back door. Why can't I drive it right over the lawn to Mrs. Cobb's?"

Aunt Hertha hestitated. "We'd wreck the grass."

I knew that. But at this time of the year and in this kind of a storm, it didn't seem to matter.

Mrs. Cobb must have agreed. "Thank heavens, you got here," she cried, bracing her door against the wind which plummeted us into her house.

She was frightened. "This is the worst I've ever seen."

She bolted the door and led us down to the basement, where we sat on blankets close to the west wall.

"Just listen to my poor house groan," she whispered hoarsely, her hand to her delicate throat. "You're supposed to open windows because of air pressure, but I just can't make myself let the rain in."

Would I ever forget the sound of that storm? It was hundreds of freight trains rolling overhead. The noise engulfed us. It couldn't be shut out.

We huddled there. Nobody talked.

Frightening. . . .

How long did we crouch in the basement? There was no way to tell. When we came out, after what seemed an eternity, the electric clocks were still motionless.

The Common was a tangle of branches, of shredded paper, and a torn sail, but nothing was actually wrecked. Down at the shoreline it might be a different story.

Mrs. Cobb urged us to stay for a supper of franks and baked beans. Naturally, this led to the subject of the cans in the lake—and who could have been so thoughtless.

"Without real evidence I can't accuse anyone of stealing," Mrs. Cobb said. "But I'll tell you in confidence that money's been missing from my house lately."

"Oh, no," I breathed.

"I've been taking precautions I never took in all my years on Loud Lake." She said fervently, "Ah, I'm glad the summer's over. I hate to be suspicious of everyone in sight . . . some of them people I've known for fifty years."

"It certainly gives you an uneasy feeling," Aunt Hertha murmured.

It occurred to Mrs. Cobb that she ought to phone The Clearing and find out if she had to report for work. "You never know," she said when we laughed at her.

It was then we discovered the telephone was dead.

Tracy flung her hands aloft. "Doesn't it seem as if the world's gone to pot when the phone goes?"

This threw us into another lengthy discussion. We tried to decide which modern electrical instrument we would elect to keep if *one* were all we could have. We argued like mad. We must have been touched by the storm.

Finally Aunt Hertha sighed. "We're just putting it off. We've got to face today sometime."

When we got in the car, I flipped on the car radio for news, and we learned that a tornado had narrowly missed us at Loud Lake. It had ripped across farms north of here, and then veered into Rockwood, where it tossed mobile homes around and unroofed the Congregational Church. Although it was too early to estimate damage, at least nine people had been hurt.

Aunt Hertha made a loud, choking sound. "The Congregational Church? That's just south of Sawyer Street."

A short while later I was in the back yard trying to salvage our swimming suits. Somehow it wasn't a complete surprise when Dan drove up in the Mengers' car. I could hardly speak, I was so happy to see him.

"Hi," I said brilliantly.

How frustrating to have Aunt Hertha rush right out

of the cottage! Couldn't she leave us alone for a moment?

"I couldn't get Loud on the phone," Dan said. "Nobody knew what had happened at the lake so I decided to investigate. Are you all right?"

"Tell us about Rockwood. Tell about Sawyer Street," Aunt Hertha burst out, wiping her hands together nervously. "What's happened to my house?"

"It's okay—so far."

Aunt Hertha looked sort of sick. "Tell me."

When Dan said *so far* that was exactly what he meant. The house was still intact, but a huge birch tree in the back yard had been uprooted. In falling, it had hit the telephone wires and snagged there. But no one could guarantee how long those wires would hold. "It's hanging over your kitchen wing," Dan told her.

That meant the laundry, a small family room, and the garage. "I don't know what my insurance covers," Aunt Hertha moaned. "I certainly don't have money for repairs. What'll I do?"

A moment of thought, and then her usual decisiveness appeared. "I'm going to Rockwood."

Tracy said, "Me too."

My aunt turned to me. "Are you coming?"

She didn't know yet that the police didn't want me to go back to Sawyer Street, and I didn't care to add to her distress now. "I wish you'd let me keep Dawn here, Aunt Hertha," I hastily volunteered. "She's already had

98

so much excitement. You and Tracy go into town and take care of everything."

"Bless you, Jenny dear." She dabbed her forehead with her handkerchief. "If there's commotion at home, it certainly would be a relief to know you're taking care of her out here. And with Mrs. Cobb so close—"

"That's right. If she can stay alone all winter at Horseshoe Park, Dawn and I can manage a couple of days—if that's what it will take you in Rockwood. You know, I've stayed here without my parents."

"Will you get word to Mrs. Cobb right away that you two are alone?"

I promised.

Now I caught Dan looking at me with a curious hesitancy. "Why don't you come, too? You could use my bedroom, and I could bunk at your house."

My eyes met his, and we exchanged a wary glance. Then I said, "Don't be silly! Dawn and I will set up classes the minute you go. We'll have a ball, won't we, sweetie?"

Dan still disapproved. When Tracy and my aunt sped into the cottage for their pocketbooks, he grabbed me by the shoulders. "I don't like this, Jenny," he said in a tight, careful voice. "I think we should let your aunt know that—"

"We'll tell her nothing," I said firmly. "Talk about *Dawn* being excitable! You should know what Aunt Hertha can be like. If we tell her what we know, she'll be in a dither—and she'll just die if she can't go back to Sawyer Street now."

He seemed about to protest further, but my aunt's appearance silenced him. She was ready to go. She'd leave her own car for me.

They had started down the driveway when, to my surprise, Dan stopped the car, leaped out again, and came running back to where I stood with Dawn. For a moment he just stared at me. Then he put one hand flat against each of my cheeks, pulling my face close to his. There was a strange urgency in his eyes. Out of our Sawyer Street childhood came his husky demand: "Put your hand on your heart, and swear till you're blue in the face. You won't be scared?"

Solemnly I put my hand over my heart. "I'm blue in the face."

Turning to my young cousin, with a note in his voice that was new to me, he said, "Take care of my girl, Dawn."

Dawn held on to my hand tightly. As they drove out of sight I was flooded with an unexpected dismay. If only they could remove the tree right away and come back! But why fool myself? If there was a lot of damage, how could Aunt Hertha find anybody to cut away the tree now?

Get involved. Get busy.

As I held open the back door for Dawn, the horn of another car sounded briefly. There was Mrs. Cobb,

100

waving, and holding one hand to her delicate throat while she drove away. She didn't know I was alone. She wasn't aware that Aunt Hertha was gone.

Tears filled my eyes. When I closed the back door I had to fight loneliness, doubt, and something that was almost terror. I wished we'd had a new lock put on when Aunt Hertha suggested it.

chapter sixteen

The afternoon was interminable. Would it ever end? As an only child I was used to solitude. I thought I liked it so much that I'd begged and begged my parents to let me stay alone during their trip. However, now I discovered that mine had been a different kind of privacy from what I had to face this afternoon.

With no telephone, no radio, no family, no neighbors —it was scary! But I had to try to hide my fears from Dawn, who managed to sense my moods even when she couldn't catch the reason for them.

Although the wind had died down it was damp and chilly in the cottage, and I decided that before I started to work with her I'd build a fire in the fireplace. A pile of wood was always kept in the half-basement off the back stairway so that it would be dry for an emergency

—and that's what this was, I thought grimly. I'd have to replace what I used from the pile outside.

There were candles. There was a large utility flashlight, which we used mainly to hunt night crawlers for fishing bait. There was a charcoal grill in the garage, so that we could have hot food.

We'd make out. "What shall we sing, Dawn?" I asked brightly.

She smiled, but she didn't speak.

Had she said anything all day? She'd been silent during our walk to Loud and, now that I thought of it, she hadn't made a sound during all the commotion of the storm, or when her mother and sister went off so suddenly without her.

The fire sulked and sank, and I nursed it until it crackled, warming the cottage with a rosy darkness. I took Dawn's hands in mine and danced her around the living room, singing:

"The farmer in the dell, the farmer in the dell,

Hi ho, the dairy oh, the farmer in the dell."

She *wanted* to enjoy herself. Yet her eyes slid away from me and searched the dark corners of the room. I watched her with a twist in my heart. The darkness was beyond her understanding. Why didn't Jenny turn on the lights? Why did the depths of the cottage writhe and flicker, and what was that dark thing that kept following her around?

"Shadow," I said. "That's called a shadow."

Her face was anxious.

"Here, sit on this stool with me and I'll show you." With my hands I made creatures on the wall, rabbits with long ears that wiggled in the firelight. "Shadow, shadow," I repeated. Drawing her face close to my head, I urged, "Whisper that word in my ear."

It felt like Christmas when I heard her whisper, "Shadow."

"Good! Now I'll tell you what we're going to do. We have such a nice fire to come back to that we'll walk down to the lake and see what happened during the storm. Then we'll fix some nice hamburgers. We'll cook them here in the fireplace. Won't that be fun?" I doubted it myself.

I put two sweaters on Dawn and tied a wool scarf around her head. I don't know why, but I decided to wear my father's worn sport jacket. There was something comforting about it.

What I really wanted to see, besides any damage, was whether or not there were lights in any nearby cottages.

Today Mrs. Cobb hadn't been able to leave her light aglow. The total darkness was a rare thing. Would she be afraid to come back to complete blackness? Would she come back?

I shivered.

We stood at the top of the long stairway. One of the rafts had broken loose and was wedged under the

Thompsons' pier to the east of us. Never had I known the water to look this uninviting. It was so motionless that it seemed dead.

Suddenly Dawn buried her face in my skirt.

"Time for supper," I said quickly. "We'll eat by the fireplace. Your job will be to put the salt and pepper on the hamburgers."

It was cold enough outside so that the cottage fire seemed warm and inviting. Really, though, what a poor weapon it would be against bitter weather. Now I had the answer to our argument at Mrs. Cobb's today. If I could only have one modern convenience my choice would be automatic heat.

Dawn swayed against the chair. She seemed hypnotized by the flames, which shot in all directions just like the shadows had. I lighted a candle and went for more wood. While I was at it I loaded my arms with logs and raced up and down to our half-basement, stacking extra wood in the back stairway for later.

The boards in the cottage creaked. The windows were squares of silver.

How I missed Aunt Hertha's chattering! If only she were here, grumbling at her cards, making plans for our every living moment. Her shrill laughter would have been music.

"There." I put the beef patties on the grill. I kept

talking to Dawn, trying to rouse her. Now the onions. "Isn't that a wonderful smell?"

It looked cozy with the old piano bench, which my mother had refinished in antique white, pushed before the fire and set with silver, two glasses of milk, and a candle.

"Oh, I forgot the napkins and here I am, sitting down already. Will you get the box of napkins, sweetie? It's on the kitchen table."

She looked at me solemnly. Then she moved towards the kitchen.

She'll come around, I thought. After she'd eaten her hamburger she would brighten. Poor kid. She had no toughness. Sometimes she looked so pale she seemed blood-drained.

I broke my hamburger in half to see if it was medium rare. Fireplace cooking was a skill that I would have to learn. "Can't you find the napkins?" I called to Dawn. "They're right on the table by Mama's deck of cards."

Silence.

How strange!

Then whimpering, that ghastly whimpering. . . .

I jumped up from the piano bench and hurried to the kitchen. In the dim light I saw my young cousin across the room, standing by the back door.

Just inside the door stood Todd Bjorkland.

I was so startled to see him that for an instant I felt my mouth twist in fear. I would have screamed if I hadn't instinctively thought of Dawn—that I mustn't allow her to be terrified.

But only for one moment was I invaded by panic. Then all I thought was, here's an end to this horrible aloneness.

"Todd," I cried out. I could have hugged him.

chapter seventeen

As soon as I spoke, Dawn aimed for me and buried her face against me. I hoped Todd would understand her shyness. "She's not comfortable with strangers," I said by way of apology.

He shrugged his shoulders. "I smelled the onions—I'm hungry."

"Well, come on in," I said. "I've made enough for three."

Fortunately I had cooked all the hamburger because I was afraid it would spoil without refrigeration. Placing two large sandwiches on a paper plate, I handed it to him. He sat down in the big swivel chair between me and the front door.

I tried to make conversation about the storm, but neither of us was especially good at small talk. My

108

glance was drawn to a tiny scar on his forehead, which seemed to move in the flickering firelight. He was dressed in the same pants and shirt he'd worn every day at the lake. I realized I'd never seen him in other clothing.

"You aren't dressed warm enough for Wisconsin." I went to the cramped closet under the stairway and pulled out an old sweater of my father's. "Mrs. Bjorkland should have told you to bring something woolly for this time of year. Or didn't she warn you that Wisconsin summers are different from California?"

Todd didn't answer, he just pulled the sweater on over his head. For the first time I envied Aunt Hertha and Tracy's gift for charging up a conversation with anyone.

"Mrs. Cobb thought you'd left. She was wishing the grass could be cut once more." I looked in the direction of the lake. All was black. "If you could help with cleaning up the Common I know she'd be grateful."

Watching the way he wolfed down the hamburgers in enormous bites, I was proud of my charcoal cooking which had threatened to be such a disaster. "If I'd known you were coming I'd have tried to make hot coffee," I told him.

I put the back of my hand against the flush on Dawn's cheek. "Come on, sweetie. We'll go to the kitchen for milk."

I didn't want to leave her alone with Todd. He ter-

109

rified her. Pressed against me, her fingers clutching my red sweater, she peeked around me at him.

I brought the bottle of milk and a glass and placed it on the pile of magazines near where he sat. "Help yourself," I said.

He drained the last of the milk. "Got any cigarettes?"

I shook my head. "None of us smokes."

Stretching himself, he thrust his hands into the pockets of his tight pants and drew out several smashed packets of cigarettes, all different brands. He inspected them carefully, and drew a worse-for-wear cigarette from a green package.

Straightening it, he hunched over towards the candle on the piano bench to get a light. He rotated himself in the swivel chair while he blew out smoke. "I'm a night smoker," he said.

"If only there were electricity! If only Mrs. Cobb would come by! If only the telephone were working!" I cried out in frustration.

Todd sort of smiled at my outburst. "A storm really makes you feel isolated, doesn't it?"

I nodded mutely. From the chest of toys near where he was sitting I took a shoe box of wooden and glass beads I'd collected. Although Dawn was slow about stringing beads, and it was a problem for her to decide what color should come next, she generally enjoyed this activity and could lose herself in it. That's what I wanted now.

110

"That's pretty," I encouraged her.

Absently Todd reached down and picked up a shoestring and started stringing, too. When Dawn began to whimper, he shot an exasperated glance at her. "Oh, shut up," he said. "If you don't want me to play with your toys, I won't."

At those words, Dawn started crying outright.

Todd looked irritated. "What's wrong with this kid?"

"Dawn is an unusual child," I explained, holding her close to me.

"Can't she talk?"

I was amazed that Tracy could have spent so much time talking to Todd without mentioning her sister's problem. "Mostly she's quiet—like you." I laughed uncomfortably. "I can imagine what a lively conversation you'd hold together."

"We've had a few," he said drily.

That was funny—I'd never seen Todd with Dawn. But I didn't like to talk about Dawn in front of her. I announced, "I'd better put her to bed."

"I'll stay for a while. I'll keep the fire up for you."

Momentarily I wanted to protest, but in a way I was grateful for his company. Perhaps he, too, disliked being alone after this terrible storm. I couldn't say no.

When I had Dawn ready for bed upstairs I listened to her prayers with a silent one of my own,

111

and added an extra blanket to her bed as I tucked her in. It would be polite to go downstairs again, but I had to stay near frightened Dawn. Besides—I was exhausted.

chapter eighteen

It was the chill that wakened me.

Stiff, uncomfortable, I stared about the bedroom, which was just visible in the early morning light. I shivered convulsively.

What was that sound? Rain! "Just what we need," I moaned.

Horseshoe Park would remain deserted. Mrs. Cobb would huddle indoors, protecting her delicate throat. Had she come home last night? I hadn't heard her car, though I seldom did.

There wasn't a sound downstairs. Todd must have gone home.

Dawn was still sleeping. That was good.

Today was Wednesday. This weekend my parents would return. I wondered what was happening at home.

Was the tree still hanging over Aunt Hertha's house? Suddenly I realized that if the tree weren't cut down, Tracy wouldn't be able to have her party. Poor Tracy —after all her planning!

"Jennifer?"

I sat up, and tried to put a smile in my voice. "Good morning, Dawn."

"You've got your dress in bed."

"I forgot to take off my clothes last night. I need a mama, don't I?"

Glancing at myself in the mirror, I shuddered. But at that moment I saw that the small light over the bed was glowing. The electricity was back! "That's something," I breathed. "We can have heat and a warm breakfast."

The fireplace was dead, the cottage was raw with cold, and Todd was sitting at the table eating an apple when, hand in hand, Dawn and I came into the kitchen. "Good morning," I said. "The electricity is back."

He scratched his fingers through his hair. "Your relatives didn't come last night," he said, sullen after an uncomfortable night.

I explained about the tree hanging over my aunt's house. "I guess she couldn't get anyone to come and cut it down yesterday." It would be taken care of immediately, and then they'd be back.

Putting water on the stove, I measured cereal. Dawn needed something hot in the morning.

Breakfast was not exactly a jolly meal.

Now that we had electricity, I placed the small radio next to Dawn, and dialed till I found a program of lively polkas. From the window ledge I took two pots of geraniums, which were in full flower, and put them in the center of the table, along with the milk carton, so that she couldn't see Todd across the table. He made her nervous.

He ate *everything*. Cereal, toast, eggs. Marmalade, milk, coffee. If anything, he was more silent than last night. Dawn wasn't much of a conversationalist, but she was superior to this young man.

Above the sound of music I chatted to her about her dolls and her bunnies. We talked about the next letter she would write for me. Her frightened, darting peeks in the direction of Todd grew fewer, but I couldn't help noticing that when he made any abrupt gesture she tensed.

Finally I couldn't help bursting out, "Todd, why is Dawn so scared of you?"

He stirred sugar into his coffee silently.

I sighed. "I guess she's not used to men—come to think of it, the only man she knows well is my father, and even I don't see much of him, he's so busy." I paused. "I'm sorry she behaves so badly with you, Todd."

Suddenly he shouted, "Don't call me that name!"

I looked at him in horror.

"My name isn't Todd," he said fiercely, standing up.

115

"Your father knows that. It's too bad you don't, and Tracy doesn't, and that Mrs. Cobb who makes it her business to know everything doesn't know it." The once quiet boy who spoke in a mumble when he spoke at all now was shouting, punctuating his speech by banging on the table. The toaster rattled; I was paralyzed.

But he kept on talking.

"Your father, the great judge! I know your father pretty well. Probably a lot better than you do."

What a strange thing to say, I thought, and suddenly I felt warm, suffocated, about to faint. I caught Dawn's frightened eyes, staring at me. I couldn't faint. I had to protect Dawn.

"What *is* your name?" I asked in a whisper. But I thought I already knew.

"Eric," he said defiantly. "Eric Schallen."

Eric Schallen. A wave of fear almost made my heart stop beating. I had to pretend to be calm! "But why did you say you were Todd Bjorkland?" I asked, in what I hoped was my normal voice.

He snorted. "The old lady told me I was. I didn't tell her."

"But you're living in their cottage."

"Got to live someplace."

"How did you get in?"

"These cottages are child's play. There isn't one where I can't walk in and out whenever I want. You almost caught me here one day when I was looking for

116

grub." His grin was sardonic. "It was so simple I got careless."

Those beat-up cigarette packages. Of course, they'd been snitched.

The rain spanked the roof. In the strained silence in the kitchen the radio announcer raved about a new lavender bubble bath.

I felt my courage draining away. There was a reason for Dawn's fear of him. I said, "You told me you'd talked with Dawn."

"I have."

"But she's been with one of us all the time."

"Not in Rockwood."

I was staggered. "You talked to her on Sawyer Street?"

"How do you think I found out you were coming to this lake?" After a moment he added the chilling words, "I was waiting here when you came."

Keeping my eyes riveted on the toast I was buttering, I tried to send my mind backwards, to the morning my parents left for Europe. After Dawn had summoned me outside with her whistle, had we talked about anything except her letter? Had she seemed frightened? *Shut up, shut up.* When had Dawn first used that phrase? For I knew now where she'd picked it up. And the bruise on her wrist—hadn't I noticed it the very day of our arrival?

I remembered how sad she'd been in the car coming

here, and her words about the man she was going to hit and bite.

The man. This was the man, and there'd been no dream, no nightmare. This was the man she'd written about in her letter before we came to Loud Lake.

How long had he been hanging around?

I knew he was watching my face. I brushed toast crumbs from my fingers with painful attention to them.

I wondered how I was going to survive.

chapter nineteen

Dread washed through me. Without Dawn I'd have dissolved, but to protect her I had to pull myself together. A funny thing. I was protecting her, but she in turn was my protection.

There was nothing I could do except pretend I was dumb, and continue to stall. After a few moments I said, "What were you doing in our neighborhood?" I rose from the table to carry the soiled dishes to the sink.

"You had a broken window, didn't you?"

"We had a pane broken in our dining room." I hung on to what composure I could manage. "We've had that before when birds tried to migrate right through our house. What does that have to do with you?"

He made a brusque sound. "When are your folks coming back?"

"My parents? Any time now."

"Don't give me that! When you fly you've got a day and an hour. There's no *any* time."

I don't know what I would have answered, but at that moment there was a quick rapping at the back door. It was so unexpected that, momentarily, I was paralyzed. Then I whirled to scream, but already he was across the room and his strong fingers made a painful barricade across the lower half of my face. With his other hand he grabbed my wrist.

Dawn just sat there, staring blankly.

Again the rapping. Mrs. Cobb's husky voice called, "Hertha?"

He didn't let go. Maneuvering me forward, he steered me into the back bedroom where the lower level of the window was chin-high. He muttered, "Tell her to go."

"Who is it?" I called stupidly.

"Oh, Jenny. Don't come outside. You'll only get wet. Tell your aunt I'm on my way to the doctor's office. My voice is about gone. The key to my back door is hanging on the flagpole in case you all need anything. But the phone isn't working yet."

With stricken eyes, I watched her scurry across the yard to her car.

Eric Schallen said brusquely, "I could take care of her too. All three of you are cream puffs."

He didn't have to tell me that. I knew it already. I swayed against the paneled wall, wet now from the rain coming in the window. "You hurt my arm," I whispered, rubbing it.

"Let's get something straight," he told me. "Don't make trouble for me, and I won't make trouble for you, until the judge comes."

"Jennifer," Dawn called in an unhappy voice.

"Coming, sweetie."

He went into the living room. To distract my cousin I coaxed her to help me clean the kitchen. With foot-high suds, she washed and rewashed our breakfast utensils, while I kept complimenting her on a splendid job. Anything to keep her occupied so that she wasn't overwhelmed by fright of "the man."

"He's naughty," she told me in a whisper.

Sprawled in front of the fireplace, Eric Schallen shaved a stick of kindling over the ashes of last night's fire. Was he showing off when he took out his knife, reminding me that he had one?

Somehow I had to find help. It was as if my mind were a vacuum. My thoughts bogged down.

I didn't even hear Eric come into the kitchen until he said, "Get your coats. We're getting out of here."

He whistled nervously while I wrapped my cousin against the chill rain. I collected her rabbits and dolls and a wool robe to tuck over her.

Eric didn't ask for the key to my aunt's car because he'd already taken it from my pocketbook. He pushed us out the back door, and when we passed the clothes-

121

line he slashed it with his knife. Unpinning the soaked towels and bathing suits, he dumped them on the garage floor.

He ordered Dawn to lie down on the back seat. Shoving me into the front seat next to him, he knotted one end of the clothesline around my wrists.

Trying to keep a quiver out of my voice, I pleaded, "Don't tie me, please," I faltered. "You ought to know you don't need a rope for me as long as you have Dawn."

Maybe he realized I spoke the truth. Nevertheless, he kept my wrists bound.

We drove to Mrs. Cobb's garage, where he picked up the empty gasoline cans that usually held fuel for the mowing machines. Then he backed up to the Bjorklands' where he took a red rubber tube about four or five feet long from his jalopy.

After that we seemed to drive around aimlessly, but I supposed there was a plan to his scouting. This part of the countryside was full of small lakes. We drove along their shores while he studied the shacks, particularly those which were boarded up for winter. He seemed attracted by the deserted ones, off the beaten track.

My heart felt like a stone inside me. In the rear-vision mirror I caught a glimpse of my face—anxious, strange, wan. I'm beginning to look like him, I thought grimly.

Now an abandoned farm aroused his interest. We

122

drove down the rutty lane so he could inspect it more thoroughly. He peered through the openings of the boarded-up windows, and then into the weathered barn, which looked as if it might sag to the ground any minute. What he thought of the place he didn't say.

As we drove he kept the radio on, switching from station to station to get news. The tornado was reported as a disastrous one. I despaired. No one in Rockwood would be concerned about us at Loud Lake, knowing that we'd escaped the destruction. They had more important things on their minds.

Suddenly he hit the steering wheel angrily. We were almost out of gas.

In a gas station, I thought, I might have a chance to signal for help. But we drove past station after station.

Finally we came to the huge parking area of a shopping center, which covered acres of former farms. There we circled until we reached the area where employees parked. He was clever. He knew the owners of these cars would not be going in and out at this time of day. We would be alone here.

Now I understood about the red rubber tube. I'd never seen gas siphoned before. He drained two cars. After the gas gauge on my aunt's car registered F he filled the gasoline cans and put them in the trunk.

I said, "You've siphoned from my car, haven't you?"

He nodded.

"At the Festival?"

123

Again he nodded. "I had the idea you'd get stuck in the country and maybe I'd get you then. But this has worked out better." He looked at me sharply. "When the judge comes back I'm going to use you for bargaining. I'm going to swap you for my brother."

So that was it. Now I felt sick. I made a despairing sound. "My father can't bargain. He wouldn't be able to release a prisoner because his daughter. . . ."

I buried my head in my hands. "Let's go back to the cottage," I begged. For some reason I felt protected there.

But when we sloshed through the puddles and pushed open the back door, it was only to meet another blow.

A white sheet of paper had been squeezed under our back door. Mrs. Cobb had written: "Hertha, sorry I missed you. I'm going to stay at my daughter's until my throat improves. My voice is gone. The telephone rang but I couldn't answer. If you want to use it, you know where my key is."

Dawn was watching my face as I read. I dared not show my anguish. She said, "Will she get a star for her letter, Jennifer?"

"A gold-star letter." Bending over, I hid my face while I freed her from her wraps. "How about some chocolate milk and then a nap?"

She nodded, too tired to agree or disagree.

Eric said, "Fix us some food. I'm hungry."

"Let me put Dawn to sleep first." He didn't object.

I crouched over her bed, patting her so she would close her eyes. They seemed starched open. She needed routine, and she wasn't getting it. I sang, "Mary, Mary, quite contrary, how does your garden grow?"

She yawned and clung to my fingers.

"Deedle, deedle, dumpling, my son John."

Her beautiful eyes glazed, then she breathed heavily.

So now—my first time alone with him without Dawn for protection. I'd talk, talk, talk. You don't strike down a friend, I thought, so I'd act friendly.

Combined with Eric's roughness was an undefined quality, which I couldn't figure out. Was it confusion? Was he slightly less than confident about all of this— or was it my need to cling to something reassuring that made me hope he wasn't as merciless as he pretended to be?

"There's some pea soup, but it'll take a little while to defrost," I said. "Or there's canned soup, mushroom or chicken noodle."

He was so hungry that he couldn't wait for anything to defrost. I had to give him a can of sardines and rye bread before I measured out the coffee.

"What's your brother's name?"

"Harland. I call him Frosty."

"Why?"

"I've forgotten."

"Have you any more family?"

125

"Nope."

I poured some milk into the mushroom soup. "If you have no family, then there's nobody to help you. So what would you do, if you actually got your brother by holding me hostage?"

"I've made plans."

"Where would you go?"

He stuffed both cheeks with bread. "It's easy to get to Canada. I've learned a few things where I've been living lately. About not leaving fingerprints. And not making the mistake of hanging around your old neighborhood where they'll be looking for you. Nobody knows where I am—except you."

His eyes slid sidewise at me. "All I gotta do is exchange you for Frosty."

I said helplessly, "Well, you—you're certainly a loyal brother."

"Loyal?" An expression I couldn't read twisted the corners of his mouth. He made a sound like a laugh, but it wasn't pleasant.

"Stoke up," he ordered. "We've got things to do while the kid sleeps."

I went silent with shock. I had to compel myself to lift my spoon to my mouth. I suppose I ate something, I can't remember.

"Come on," he ordered, and he threw my damp coat at me.

126

chapter twenty

First he marched me to the edge of the bluff. He ordered me to stand on the top step, hands in my pockets, and gaze downwards. "What do you think would happen to the kid if she accidentally fell all the way to the bottom? It could happen, you know. She's awkward."

Absolutely speechless, I backed away until I bumped into the bench. My eyes stung. I forced out, *"Please."*

"You're really nervous about her, aren't you?"

I nodded.

"Okay. Now we understand each other. Now you're going to telephone."

On the flagpole we found the key where Mrs. Cobb said it would be. Her house was warm, and it smelled of oranges. Her kitchen phone hung above a pine breakfast bar which covered an old-fashioned radiator. Her collection of cookbooks and her milk-glass apothecary jars stood in the open cupboard with the old clock that chimed the hour of five as we entered the room.

Eric commanded, "Call your aunt and tell her you're okay. I don't want her coming back and lousing up my plans." His fingers bit into my shoulder. "I'll be listening to every word."

I whispered in a sick voice, "Yes, I know," and then I dialed.

My mind churned. Wasn't there something I could say that would alert my aunt? If I weren't so desperately tired I wouldn't be so blank. Wasn't there a signal she would understand?

I heard Tracy's voice. "Hello?"

"Hi," I said. "I'm phoning because Mrs. Cobb has lost her voice."

Tracy laughed. "Wouldn't you know!" How wonderful she sounded, this cousin of mine whom I'd avoided all these years. "That's why we didn't get an answer when we called. Mom was beginning to worry. Are you all right?"

I nodded, squeezing back tears. I couldn't make the words come.

"Jenny?" she called, her voice carrying so clearly that I knew Eric could hear her. He was standing close to me, his head inclined towards the receiver. He nudged my back.

128

I gulped. "How about the tree? How about your house? How about Rockwood?"

"Oh, Rockwood's a mess. . . ." Then came a torrent of words. I could picture her with arms waving wildly, acting out the tornado, throwing houses and mobile homes around like matchboxes. Her arms were probably closing the schools until next week, lifting off the roof of the Congregational Church. The exercise she got!

I interrupted with, "You haven't told me about the tree yet."

"It's still hanging over us. Mom can't find a single workman who isn't busy."

I clung to Mrs. Cobb's kitchen stool. "How's Dan?"

"He's sleeping at your house."

"Why?"

"Your dining-room window was broken. And it wasn't the storm, or a bird. Somebody threw a rock through it, Jenny. Dan told us the police are looking for a guy who broke out of prison. Don't worry—but we're sure glad that you're at Loud Lake."

Now my shoulder was pinched. I was being told that I'd talked long enough. But I couldn't bring myself to say good-bye. Almost feverishly I said, "I'll bake your fortune cake like I promised. Mrs. Cobb can't bring it but I'll think of something."

"Oh, Jenny, my party's off—the storm ruined that along with everything else. But that's sweet of you."

129

I closed my eyes. "Tell Dan—tell him—"

By this time Eric was twisting my arm. "Good-bye," I said. "Good-bye, Tracy."

While we walked across the dreary Common I told Eric about the fortune cake. I shivered—he might have been invited to this party. Back in the cottage, I pulled the little metal trinkets from their storage place on the top shelf and let him examine them.

At that moment the fortune cake seemed my only link to Sawyer Street.

"I'll polish them tonight," I said. "Dawn can help me. It'll give her something to do."

He scratched his head. "That's a lot of trouble for nothing. Even if you bake a cake, who's going to take it to her?"

Sitting there at the kitchen table he let the small trinkets fall through his fingers and bounce on the table.

I persisted, "You seem to get such a kick out of throwing stones at the judge's house. We can take the cake into town and you can break another window."

"Shut up!"

"Why do you do it, anyway? You got your message across with the first stone."

He shrugged. Then he grinned, and for a minute he was ten years old. "It's fun."

Outside a gust of wind threw wet drops against the windowpanes. Aimlessly I cleaned up the kitchen, hardly knowing what I was doing. I used cleanser on the

130

trinkets, then lined them along the windowsill to dry. Baking the cake could be a waste of time, a complete waste, but in my desperation I clung to it as the only possible means of communicating for help. I could think of nothing else.

Eric Schallen had his nightly smoke. I tried to sew. Clumsily, I stabbed myself with the needle. Finger to mouth, I looked up and saw him staring at me.

"You're put together real good," he said, running his eyes over my figure.

I blushed, and I hated myself for reacting. I *had* to hide my dismay. Almost frantically I went back to my sewing. I couldn't let him know how he'd staggered me. If he touched me I—I'd—

"Do you have a girl friend?" I was proud of how natural my voice sounded.

"I had one once, but Frosty got to liking her, and. . . ."

Keep him talking, keep him talking. There was something about his brother that seemed to need airing. Ask him questions about his childhood, his mother. Did he like sports in school? Oh? He was good at scrub ball? What was scrub ball? It was only when he drifted back to the subject of Frosty, which he did as if drawn by invisible strings, that his face changed. It became a mask of a face, a sad mask.

That was a quiet, dark, ghastly evening.

In the night Dawn was fretful, and her whimpering

131

woke me. She was crying in her sleep. Desperate, frightened, I lay down beside her and held her in my arms. After what seemed an eternity, she relaxed and grew quiet again.

Silently I opened the bedroom door and tiptoed out into the hallway. From down in the living room came the sound of heavy snoring. Peering down the stairs, I could see that Eric had pushed the swivel chair against the bottom of the stairway to block it. He had combined the chair with the small divan to make a bed for himself. He lay with his head thrown back and, sleeping, I could stare at him as I dared not do when he was awake.

What surprised me was how very young he looked.

Forgetting myself, I leaned forward too far and a floorboard squeaked. Instantly the snores ceased. Even in sleep he was on guard.

I slumped back against the wall, breathless. For the first time since I'd been taken hostage, tears squeezed through my tightly shut eyelids. I'd been afraid to cry. I'd been afraid I'd never stop.

Well, Tracy, I thought. I've had to come to grips with unpleasantness that my parents couldn't prevent. The NO TRESPASSING sign got knocked down. How've I done, Tracy? You said I didn't have guts. You said I didn't know about the treadmill of caring for one like your sister. You were right; but I know now.

Downstairs . . . again the rhythm of deep sleep.

I crept back to Dawn.

132

chapter twenty-one

It was early, early Thursday. Eric was restless.

"If you insist, go ahead and bake your silly cake, but get it done while I eat breakfast," he said, blowing at his coffee to cool it. "I want to get going."

What did he mean? I didn't ask.

The rain had ceased and the dawn revealed a clammy and uninviting world. On the top branches of the oaks, crows screamed at each other. Wet leaves were plastered against the screens on the porch and there'd be sloppy walking underfoot if you stepped on the Common.

The eastern sky was streaked with dazzling vividness, indicating that finally we might be seeing the sun. My mind was a constant prayer . . . please, sun, show yourself! If the sun came out, the regulars were more liable to return to the lake. Tomorrow was Friday, the beginning of the weekend.

"Fix the works," he ordered when I asked him what he wanted for breakfast. Surly, nervous, he again played with his knife and the fireplace wood.

The treadmill of keeping Dawn occupied began again. "Your letter, sweetie. Here's your paper and pencil. You write me about the ride in the car yesterday, while I bake a cake for Tracy."

It would have to be a box cake. There was a chocolate mix, and a yellow cake mix on the shelf. "I'll make a marble cake," I said.

Cramming toast in his mouth, Eric shook his head over my persistence.

I said in a light, breathless voice, "I always doctor up a cake mix. Another egg, butter. . . ." Turning my back to him, I started the electric mixer and dumped spices into the batter.

Spices—that I didn't mention. Something that would say to the person tasting it: this is more than a cake! This must be a message! Garlic? No, that would smell during baking. What flavor in a birthday cake would arouse curiosity? I searched the shelf. Ah . . . *mustard*.

"And now, the fortune symbols," I murmured.

Into the oven. I poured more coffee for Eric, which he carried into the living room. He stood looking out the window. He was edgier than yesterday. As my father's return grew closer, was he quite as determined?

Was his bravado wearing thin with time? I didn't know.

Leaning over Dawn's shoulder, I murmured, "Nice, dear."

She had written: "We went to a old house. We looked in the window of a old house. It was a farm. No cows. No pigs."

"On Lake Mary," I whispered. "Can you write that?"

"I can write that," she said proudly.

"Haven't you forgotten about the man?"

"How do you spell him?"

"*E - R - I - C.*"

Her long lashes swept upwards and her eyes glowed.

"This will be a gold-star letter," I told her.

The cake had to bake forty-five minutes, so I poured coffee for myself and dawdled over it. Eric went from window to window, staring out at the Common. There was a sullen restlessness about him.

Finally his patience came to an end. Cake or no cake, we had things to do. He ordered me to put on my sweater. "Tell the kid we're going to the other cottages. I don't want her tagging along."

"But I can't leave her alone."

"*Tell her.*"

It was amazing what an inventive mind I had, when I was trying to keep Dawn from growing frightened. I told her the cake needed ten more min-

135

utes, and I showed her that I was setting the kitchen timer. Then I turned off the heat, but left the cake in the oven.

"It will be your job to listen for the bell," I said. "When it rings you must blow your whistle, so I can come and take the cake out of the oven." She could stand on the front porch and watch for me. "That's your job," I repeated, making it sound important.

I set the timer for its limit of one hour. Just so Dawn thought she was standing there for a definite period, she would be patient.

To my distress Eric knotted the clothesline around my waist and secured the other end to his belt. If my face revealed my unhappiness it didn't bend his will.

Believe me, that Thursday morning was an education. We broke into cottage after cottage on the Common to raid the kitchen shelves. Only at the Elemons' was Eric forced to break a pane and reach inside to unlock the door.

We couldn't have found a better supply of food in a supermarket. Loading my arms, he took all that he and I could carry to his jalopy in the Bjorklands' garage. His only precaution, as far as I could see, was that instead of trudging straight across the Common he made us circle in back of the cottages.

"Nobody's around," he said, "but why take a chance?"

It surprised me that it was his old car he was loading

136

up. I would have thought he'd take a modern one like my aunt's. But he'd thought that out too. "The cops won't be on the alert for a wreck like this," he said, kicking a tire.

Whenever I could, I waved to the little white face pressed against the windowpane.

"Dump those cans in the back seat," Eric ordered.

I cooperated. "I don't know why you don't put them in the trunk."

When he glanced around at me there was a curl to his mouth. "I need the space in the trunk for something else," he said brusquely.

I went hollow inside.

Now he ransacked the Bjorkland cottage for blankets and pillows and kitchenware. There was no doubt in my mind, he was taking us away from Loud Lake. My heart was pounding, but I forced myself to talk.

"Where did you get this car?" I asked.

"It was the first one I found with the keys hanging in the lock," he told me. "Not much to look at, is it?"

"With all that food, and with the way you get gas, you could get to Canada without spending a cent," I suggested.

He gave me an appraising look. "We'll wait for the judge. I'll give him a choice. You—or Frosty. It'll be up to him what happens."

His brows drew together. "One more thing," and he led me to the bluff, then down the stairway to our boat.

Loosening it, he shoved it out in the water. "This will give 'em something to think about. Your empty boat, and you gone—with your car in the garage. They'll have to drag the whole lake."

He seemed proud of himself. In fact, he was now so relaxed that he decided we'd have time for one more hot meal here at the cottage.

After our morning of work he was whistling between his teeth when he snapped on the radio to listen to the news. I prepared hamburgers from the ground meat we'd swiped at the Laudmans'.

I patted the meat. While it was cooking I threw together a boxed icing, stiffening it with powdered sugar. I worked at the sink so he needn't be conscious of what I was doing, for plainly he was annoyed by my insistence on baking the cake. My two cake layers were nothing to be proud of, but I carefully adjusted one on top of the other and iced them together lavishly, swirling the last spoonful into a peak in the middle, so that my culinary effort looked quite magnificent when I'd finished with it.

"Pretty," Dawn said.

I smiled at her. "Will you draw a big sign for me, sweetie? I'll spell. CHEW CAREFULLY. We wouldn't want Tracy to swallow her fortune."

It pleased her to be of assistance. Watching her laboriously construct each letter, I was overwhelmed by a frantic affection for her. At that moment I could have

138

squared off to the world in her defense. What a crazy time to feel this vast surge of love!

By this time I'd overcooked the meat. I braced myself for what Eric might say when he bit into it, but he was so deep in thought he hardly seemed to notice what he was eating.

Suddenly, however, he looked at me with those unrevealing eyes of his. He jumped to his feet. "Come on, we're getting out." We'd overstayed our time in this cottage, he said irritably. It would be just his luck to have somebody charge in here before we left. We'd go —pronto!

He wouldn't let me wash the dishes. He wouldn't let me carry the cake down to Mrs. Cobb's. He was nervous and testy. "I told you that cake was a waste of time."

There was such tension building in him to flee this place that he buzzed with it. Yet because Dawn and I had become individuals instead of anonymous pawns, he allowed me the time to collect toys for Dawn, and he even carried her dolls and bunnies to the Bjorklands' garage.

Then the escaped convict took over.

He forced his hostages into the trunk, locked it, and drove away from Horseshoe Park.

chapter twenty-two

The farmhouse stood at the end of a long rutty driveway, in a wild ragged setting of woods and partial clearing. It belonged there, like the elderberry bushes, the hemlocks, the squirrels, and the woodchucks, and like algae-covered Lake Mary, which wasn't more than a drainage pond despite the dignity of its name.

Unpainted, stark, and boxlike, with a high roof, the house had all the sadness of a place unvisited and in decay. It looked as if nobody had wandered this way since the day the last occupant had boarded the windows on the ground floor and abandoned the house.

A large barn sagged behind the house. Eric put his old car in the barn. When we started unloading our stolen supplies to take into the house he kept looking upward suspiciously, as if he expected the entire roof to collapse on us. We whispered. It was that kind of a place. When we pushed into the empty house there were whispery sounds, in the walls, in the eaves.

Our footsteps echoed.

Comforts? None. I wondered if he'd thought this out. Would we be using the soft drinks we'd taken from the cottages to wash our teeth? Outdoor plumbing? *That* would be something!

"Well, at least there aren't Indians," I offered hoarsely, "though I keep thinking I see things moving behind trees."

He glared at me. "Shut up," came from between his teeth.

At that, Dawn lifted her chin. "You *naughty,*" she accused him.

It was so unexpected it set us both back. Then, as a redness rose in his face, I swept her into a bear hug and held her close to protect her from his wrath. "That's right, sweetie. But he won't say those words again."

This man had been sentenced to prison for murder, I reminded myself. Be careful! Don't annoy him. Especially now when his nerves were wearing thin. There'd been too much time for him to think. This scheme was taking an unbearably long time to execute.

I prayed he wouldn't do anything rash.

I'd noticed that he liked to think that he was good

141

at planning. "You certainly picked a spot," I said now. "Who'd ever think you could find a lonesome place like this!"

And I started on an inspection tour of my latest prison as if I were really interested in what he'd produced for us. The first floor had a kitchen, a dining room, and two parlors. We had dumped our equipment in the back parlor. Now I stuck my head through the door into the small front one. "Dawn and I'll set up classes in here," I said. "But I'm thirsty. Can't we have a soft drink? And those cookies we found at the Elemons' looked good."

He welcomed the distraction. "We should have brought your cake."

My fortune cake! I tried to keep my composure. Had anybody come to Horseshoe Park yet?

He tossed a box of cookies to me. "Catch."

It was a friendly gesture, and I smiled. Sometimes I could almost forget this painful situation, and believe he was awkward, shy Todd Bjorkland.

In the front parlor Dawn and I made ourselves as comfortable as possible on the lower ledge of a rusted, iron plant stand of the stepladder design. There was nothing else her size.

How quiet it was! Without any customary noise, like the radio, this dead silence seemed unnatural. I never knew before that I gulped so loudly when I swallowed. I could hear my own breathing.

142

Unexpectedly Eric made an impatient grunt. "A can opener! Did I forget—" and he clattered towards the kitchen, his heels coming down hard on the bare boards. There followed the sounds of searching.

Closing my eyes, I concentrated on my parents. Where were they now? Were they packing for the homeward trip? I thought of Dan. *Help me. . . .*

I felt myself beginning to crack. The hot tears would turn on, unless I caught hold of myself.

Dawn sipped her lemon soda slowly. Drinking from the bottle was a new experience. She slopped it over her face, but that hardly mattered.

Going aimlessly from one boarded-up window to the other, I peered through the cracks. What a strange way to spend a Thursday afternoon in September!

I began studying the wallpaper. The design was made up of dozens and dozens of tiny rosebuds. No garden ever grew that many rosebuds.

"Dawn, I've got an idea. Where are your colors? Where's your pencil?"

"I need the pencil," Eric said, coming into the room with a torn paper sack in his hand.

He took the pencil, and we settled for the colors.

While I coaxed Dawn into using the wallpaper as a blackboard, he slouched down on the floor so far he seemed to be sitting on his shoulder blades. He composed a threatening note to my father, asking me how to spell such words as *hostage.*

143

It took Dawn a while to overcome her feeling that we were doing something naughty by drawing on the walls, but then she grew absolutely delighted with this novelty. She was having more fun than she'd had since we'd come to Loud Lake.

I drew a bunny. She colored it blue. I drew heads with hair and ears. We put in one face that laughed. We put in a face that cried. Then we tried a face called Halloween, which was all big teeth. I drew one side of a road, up and down and around. She tried to follow my pathway, making the other side of the road, slowly, painstakingly.

"I'll play you a game of boxes," I suggested to Eric. "Huh?"

I drew a big square, eleven rosebuds across and eleven down. "Didn't you ever play boxes when you were little? You take turns drawing a line to connect the rosebuds. You try to complete a box, and when you do we put your initials in the square. Whoever finishes the most boxes wins. Come on," I urged, somewhat wildly, "are you scared I'll beat you?"

There was a frown on his face when he drew his first line from rosebud to rosebud. In his uncertainty, he actually reminded me of Dawn. However, he really must have been bored, because even the competition of this child's game excited him.

A fantastic afternoon.

We went from boxes to tic-tac-toe. While we covered

the walls of that front parlor with our scrawlings, we even laughed and chattered. Eric made a house at one end of Dawn's road and he drew a church for her at the other end. He made little people, and horses, and cows, and sheep, going down the road to church. He had a real knack for drawing, and when Dawn showed her pleasure he liked it. Lo and behold, he blossomed from a taciturn lout into fairly decent company.

He began reminiscing about the fun he and Frosty used to have while their mother was alive. After she died his father changed, and life became a bitter battle between Frosty and the old man.

"Did they have tempers, both of 'em! You should've heard them going at it over who was going to use the car." He shook his head as if he couldn't believe what he remembered. "Frosty'd get so mad I thought he'd bust."

It could be that Eric never had enjoyed quite such an interested listener as he had in me that Thursday afternoon. He luxuriated in it. He gloated over past incidents that illustrated what a staunch alliance he and his brother had, how they could depend on each other . . . it was Eric and Frosty against *everybody*. I suspected he was doctoring the tales to prove his point, but I pretended I believed, and I kept throwing out just enough questions to keep him talking.

Frosty, the roof over his head. Frosty, the ground under his feet. For Frosty, he'd do *anything*. . . .

That I did believe. He craved his brother's approval. Frosty had been the leader in their adventures, and part of the reason he clung to this scheme to barter a hostage for a prisoner must be his yearning for his brother's respect.

Somehow I couldn't see Eric Schallen murdering his father. It was Frosty who had the temper. Who was violent. Who fought for the use of the car. Who hated, *hated*. . . .

Dusk had come, and I was conscious that this deserted farmhouse was without facilities of any kind. Of course, September wasn't a bitter month. But after rainy weather it could become mighty damp inside an unheated building. We had brought candles when we were scrounging supplies, but they wouldn't keep us warm.

In the dimness I glanced obliquely at the gaunt young man with the prominent cheekbones, who seemed all arms and legs. His sand-colored hair hung over his face as he drew another picture around the rosebuds, to please himself, now, for he had graduated from the kindergarten stuff he'd drawn for Dawn.

And what was he doodling? A grave. And what next? Guns, guns, guns.

I'd been fooling myself. Now I knew with a clarity I had never known before that my life was in danger. Something seemed to give way in me. My mind was a kaleidoscope of memories—Eric's history of petty crimes, his record in the juvenile systems where programs of rehabilitation had done him no good, his murder conviction.

His anger at my father, who had sent him to criminal court, had found expression in that hideous painted stone, which he had flung through our dining-room window. I bit my lip, feeling as though I'd been hit in the stomach.

I dropped my face in my hands. Back at the cottage, was anything happening? Had anybody come to Horseshoe Park and been aroused by our absence? If so, could they figure out where we were—in time to help us?

Eric made a sound when he saw me sitting there with my face in my hands. "I've got a headache," I said. "Something to eat would help. How do you like your soup? Cold, or cold?"

Unexpectedly Dawn cried out, "Let's go home, Jennifer."

"Shut up," Eric said with annoyance.

That was the spark that ignited a fire. Dawn sprang at Eric, and sank her teeth into his hand.

For a moment there was a terrifying silence.

Then he roared with rage. When I tried to push in front of Dawn to protect her he shoved me to the floor. Seizing her by the shoulders, he thrust her up the stairway to the second floor and slammed the door on her, and when she began screaming in the dark that only seemed to stimulate him.

He turned around and gave me a slow, somber look. "I've been good to you. I haven't tried anything with you . . . but now I'm done playing around."

I couldn't bear the sounds Dawn was making. Springing past Eric, I started towards the stairway, but he seized me and shook me, in a frenzy. Then he grabbed the clothesline that he always kept handy and knotted my wrists together. At last my self-possession deserted me. Helpless in this deserted house, with Dawn's screams ringing in my ears, I began to sob hysterically.

At that moment another sound pierced the emptiness of this abandoned farm.

Momentarily Eric stood, stunned—then he ran for the back door.

chapter twenty-three

The horn of Eric's jalopy was blaring—the way it had the night at Loud Lake when the short in his car woke us all up. It hadn't taken him long to fix it that night, I remembered.

But he had to make his way to the barn. I gave a convulsive jerk to the rope—no luck. It held. Well, there wasn't time to struggle with it.

I used my mouth to open the door to the stairway. "Hush," I said to Dawn, and she was so glad to see me that she did. "Come on, *hurry.*"

However, there wasn't going to be time to escape. Already came the rush of footsteps through the back entry to the kitchen.

I went rigid. I couldn't have cried—I couldn't have screamed—

149

But I did both when Dan came plunging through the back door. He had the baseball bat from the cottage in one hand, and he was gripping it fiercely. "Are you all right?" he asked in a voice I'd never heard before. His eyes were searching, intent, and they reflected his dread of asking a question that might have an unhappy answer.

I nodded mutely.

For a moment he seemed unable to move.

Then he heaved a sigh. "I need this," he said, untying the clothesline around my wrists. "Be back in a minute," he told me, and in the dark I could see his teeth set in a grim smile.

Running outside, he whistled piercingly. At his whistle the car horn ceased.

Dawn was still crying, and for the next few moments I held her close to me, comforting her. Then Dan hurried into the house again.

In the dimness I saw his face begin to work, then he pulled me tight against him, smothering me. "Jenny, Jenny." When he put his face down to mine, our cheeks were moist, and I didn't know if the tears were his, or mine, or both.

Tracy came. She threw her arms around me and we clung together.

How I loved my cousin at that moment! All during our days together at Loud Lake we'd been making up like children after spatting. Living in the cottage to-

150

gether had forced us into friendship. Now there was an explosion of affection between us.

Those next few moments were so confusing that afterwards I couldn't have described them.

We all talked.

It hadn't been a short in the horn that had sent Eric running out of the house. It was Tracy holding her fist down on the horn button. That was all she and Dan had been able to think of. Searching, hurrying, discovering this abandoned farmhouse, they weren't prepared to meet a man who might be armed. If they could lure Eric out of the dark house, they thought, they might be able to handle him.

The baseball bat had been weapon enough.

Then, when Dan whistled to Tracy that all was well, he had tied Eric with the clothesline and hurried back inside.

"But why did you go to the cottage in the first place?" I asked.

It was Mrs. Cobb who had set their search in motion, they told me. Late that afternoon she had driven out to her home, not yet aware that anything was amiss at our cottage. In fact, she didn't even know that Aunt Hertha and Tracy had been forced to return to Rockwood because of the storm damage.

Scanning the lake as was her habit, she noticed that our boat was loose and banging against the pier. When she walked up to our cottage to alert us, she found the doors open and the place empty. She called Aunt Hertha immediately.

"Eric figured it was a crafty scheme to have an empty boat on the lake and the car still in the garage," I said, with a hiccough. "I guess he imagined divers out there searching for two drowned girls, and giving him lots of time to work out his plan."

"And that might have happened," Tracy told me, "except when Dan and I reached the cottage we felt there was something mighty, mighty peculiar about that birthday cake after I positively told you there wouldn't be a party. There it stood on the kitchen table, not even covered, with a sign saying CHEW CAREFULLY."

Dawn said, "I did it, I did it."

I breathed a prayer of something like gratitude, something like thanksgiving.

"So you chewed carefully—"

"One nibble! Jennifer Lou Jonsson, you are the lousiest birthday cake baker in the world!"

"The mustard! I wanted it to taste foul."

"We knew right away it had to be *something* besides a cake. So we pulled it apart."

Thus discovering Dawn's letter to me, which I'd managed to hide between the layers when I'd slathered on the icing. It wouldn't have been possible for me to write anything with Eric watching my movements. But it never had occurred to him to check on Dawn.

Dan said, "That told the story. Eric. The old farm-

152

house with no pigs, no cows, on Lake Mary. We didn't wait. While Aunt Hertha called the police, Tracy and I took off for Lake Mary."

Just then we heard the police car, and we stumbled from the old farmhouse to meet them. For the first time there was enough light to see each other. I was shivering, but I felt both light-headed and lighthearted.

Suddenly I heard Tracy make a strangled sound. She was staring at Eric, lying outside the house, his hands and feet bound. For the first time she saw his face. "Why, Eric is—is Todd Bjorkland!"

chapter twenty-four

We drove back to Horseshoe Park and picked up Mrs. Cobb. She came to Rockwood with us, because she was so appalled at what had happened right under her unseeing eyes that she felt an absolute need for our company.

We sat around Aunt Hertha's kitchen table, drinking coffee and finishing a loaf of my aunt's banana nut bread. Everybody talked. Now that Eric was exposed, it was funny the way they'd all been suspicious of him from the first. "I knew he was odd," Tracy said, her hands swooping as she recalled our days at Loud Lake, "but he was sort of nice."

I knew exactly how she felt.

Even while Aunt Hertha and Mrs. Cobb built a case against the young man who'd never really fit in at

154

Horseshoe Park, I couldn't quite go along with the verdict.

I'd spent a lot of time with Eric. There was a side to him that they didn't know.

I remembered him shouting, "I've been good to you," and in his way he had, except at the very end.

He'd shown remarkable patience with Dawn.

He hadn't molested me. He'd said I was pretty, but he'd left it at that. I remembered with a pang that the only girl he'd cared about had preferred his brother.

Where this big brother was concerned Eric was totally naive. He worshipped Frosty. I thought of how mortified he must be now that Frosty would learn how he had botched the plans for their escape.

Suddenly I covered my face with my hands. Eric's father *was* murdered, I reminded myself. Eric *did* confess. He did throw that obscene rock, and he was proud of it.

Aunt Hertha's voice broke into my thoughts. She was gazing out her kitchen window at the darkened yard where the huge tree lay. The telephone company had eased it down today and left it to be sawed into fireplace logs. "Tomorrow we'll have to go out to the cottage and clean up before your parents come."

"Not me," I said, shuddering. "I'm not going to Horseshoe Park again—never!

The next afternoon I went to Horseshoe Park.

Dan took me. "Get it over with," he insisted.

Loud Lake was still deserted, but it was a gorgeous day. We were drawn to the patch of sunlight on the long bench over the bluff. The water was quiet, the sky and the lake painted the same hazy shade of charcoal blue, and there was a riot of fall flowers in front of the cottages.

Reaching out, I brushed aside a silken thread, and tiny spiders sailed almost invisibly through the autumn air. Overhead the crows screamed at each other and around us the squirrels were busy storing acorns.

Quite to my surprise, Dan pulled a small white box out of his pocket. Inside was a tiny silver pendant on a silver chain. Then he hung it around my neck. "Will you wear it—always?"

We stared at each other, and I could feel the pink tingling my cheeks. "In this age of airplanes," he said, "separation isn't forever." Then he kissed me. "Jenny, Jenny."

We sat there while a boat sailed all the way across Loud Lake. Then Dan said, "How about getting us a soft drink from the refrigerator, Jenny?"

"Aren't you coming too?" I didn't want to go into the cottage alone—I didn't.

"I'll wait here."

So I crossed the Common, knowing Dan was watching. I pushed at the screen door and walked in. Seconds later, screaming, I fled.

Dan raced across the Common. We met halfway. "Jenny!" He threw his arms around me. "You're hysterical."

I dug into his chest. "A mouse!"

"Oh, no!" Dan laughed. "Well, if it eats your fortune cake, it will need mouse medicare."

chapter twenty-five

"Dear Cousin, It is rainy today. I ate some oatmeal with a banana on it.

"I go to school in a church. My mama helps a teacher. I am a student. We are 4 students. In a church.

"My sister Tracy Thane had a birthday. She had a party. My cousin Jennifer Jonsson made a cake. It had a fortune in it. CHEW CAREFULLY. My fortune was a whistle.

"My aunt and my uncle were in an airplane. They came back.

"As my letter is getting long I will close. From your cousin, Dawn Thane."

It would probably be my last letter from her. As I tucked it in my pocketbook, an autumn sadness hit me.

I was packing my gear in our car. Soon my parents

would drive me to Madison, to the university. Dan was gone—he had left for college yesterday morning. But before he'd left I'd been able to give him the news that my mixed feelings about Eric Schallen were turning out to be justified.

There was going to be a complete review of his case. When the police had taken him to jail after Dan tied him up, he had broken down and told them quite a different story from the one he'd told in court.

According to Eric, it had been Frosty, in one of his violent rages, who had shot their sleeping father. Eric hadn't even been in the house at the time. He'd been horrified when he came home, but Frosty had persuaded him to help in the burial.

His brother controlled him. "He'd do *anything* for Frosty," I'd told my father.

That hero worship had helped bring Eric to the juvenile courts so often. Frosty was a wretched example for a young boy, but he was clever and didn't get caught. His younger brother, imitating him, wasn't so lucky.

It had been Frosty's idea that Eric say *he* was the killer because, at his age, he'd get off easy in juvenile court. Of course, they'd both probably have to serve some time. But they'd get it out of the way, then they'd go someplace together and start over again—that's what Frosty promised.

"Then I waived jurisdiction," my father said.

Never would I forget the horror on my parents' faces

159

when they'd learned about my hours with Eric Schallen. How glad I was, how glad, that it was all over before they stepped off the plane! And Eric? He must have had second thoughts about allowing his brother to run his life. By luck, he might have stumbled into a chance to go straight. I hoped so.

Soon I'd be in Madison, starting a new life myself. Dreamily I played with the tiny silver pendant I'd wear always, then went back to my packing.

160